AN ELEGY FOR SEPTEMBER

John Nichols

BALLANTINE BOOKS • NEW YORK

Copyright © 1992 by John Treadwell Nichols

Grateful acknowledgment is made for permission to quote "Casey Jones." Words by Robert Hunter. Copyright © 1970 by Ice Nine Publishing Company, Inc.

Library of Congress Catalog Card Number: 91-40014

ISBN: 0-345-37994-2

This edition published by arrangement with Henry Holt and Company, Inc.

Manufactured in the United States of America

First Ballantine Books Edition: August 1993

*. . . not to know and love the trag-
edy of your own life, is not to know
the joy of being here at all.*

—WALTER LOWENFELS

AN ELEGY
FOR SEPTEMBER

One

He parked the truck in front of a bulldozed mound closing off the old timber road, folded the topo map and fit it in his back pocket, dropped an apple and a few shells into the knapsack, placed three extra shells in his right front pocket, fitted a cap on his head, and began walking.

He had been tempted to bring along the letter he'd picked up on the way out, but decided against it. No intrusions this afternoon. And anyway, as always with her, after a single quick reading, he almost knew it by heart.

An ATV had been along the road, probably used by sheepherders farther up the canyon. He was disappointed by the grass it had crushed. More than anything, he wanted to feel entirely alone.

Like all secondary roads in the area, this one had been blocked off to vehicular traffic for twenty years. The road led down to a small river where clusters of golden asters made bright both sides of the stream. Timbers from an old bridge had collapsed into the water. Three little brown trout scurried for cover as he balanced across the rotting vigas and headed uphill along a tiny feeder rivulet.

Thunder rumbled, and it was clouding up down south. His road followed the water, climbing for almost two miles at a tolerable incline. On the steep slope to his left aspens were turning gold. On the right were large spruce trees. Grass en route reached almost to his knees.

He traveled two miles in the canyon shadow. Many aspen leaves were floating down, yet the air remained very quiet. When lightning lit up the sky, he flinched, but it was still far away. Nevertheless, he pointed the L.C. Smith straight down at his right side, hoping it would be less of an attraction to errant electricity.

The miniature stream burbled between large mossy rocks and moss-covered rotten logs and vegetation, which included monkshood, some alders and box elders, and swatches of dwarf bramble, much of it golden already and sporting red raspberry-like fruits.

Up higher it began to sprinkle. He crossed the creek, rousing a water ouzel, which seemed unafraid and only fluttered on to the next pool. A sweet little brook, he thought, but too small for trout. The entire sky was now overcast, thunder bursting closer each time. He cringed but continued walking. Surrounded by so many trees, how could a single strand of fire pick him out?

He assumed, given his heart, that if hit he would surely die, and hoped it would be quick. He didn't want to lie on the ground for a long time, in excruciating pain, with his hair and clothing aflame.

Then he laughed out loud. "Go for it, feel sorry for yourself, come on—let's see you *really* suffer!"

He reached a plateau where the white clover that grouse liked grew everywhere. Also kinnikin-nick, another of their favorite foods. Old logging roads crisscrossed in all directions among stands of spruce, Douglas fir, and young aspens. Little seeps and larger springs made the grass spongy, almost swampy in places.

Finally the rumble overhead became so persistent, and the fine rain so chilling, he sought refuge up a slope in an alcove created by evergreens, scrub oak, and several large aspens. For fifteen minutes he crouched there in hiding from wind, thunder, and lightning, barely getting wet. He faced downhill toward the road, where many wheat-colored strands of grass swayed in the erratic gusts. Yellow aspen leaves descended in flurries time and again, blasted off their limbs by loud outbursts of noisy air.

His safe haven was comfortable. He noticed girdles of moss at the base of aspen and spruce alike. Also, kinnikinnick, some thimbleberry, and the delicate heart-shaped leaves of Canadian violets. Trees that had fallen nearby were covered by moss and leaves, engorged by the forest. He wondered how long the process had taken.

While the rain continued, he took his pulse, checking out the heartbeat. Everything seemed okay inside, no trace of fibrillation.

"Dearest Mister _____," her initial fan letter had begun almost three months ago. She claimed to love him because his books were mighty special. As always he had written back politely, urging caution. But that didn't stop her at all. Letters began rolling in, often twice a week. In them she poured her heart out. At first, he had answered sparely, in subdued tones, intrigued but wary. She was only a junior in college, the same age as his daughter. Yet she was articulate, funny, sexy, obnoxious—mercurial. Furthermore, she had applied for, and received, a three-week writing residency at the Rhinehart Center, a local arts foundation. So they were destined to meet.

"D-Day is September FOURTH!" she had announced two months ago.

"September is my vacation," he wrote back, "and I desperately need the break."

"I'll give you a break," came her immediate answer. "I'll fuck your socks off! You'll never know what hit you! We can *fly* together!"

"Fly?" he scoffed, eager to avoid the trap. "I can hardly *walk*. I'm sick, I got no energy, my heart is a mess, I'm in the middle of a divorce, I'm broke, I live in a two-room apartment the size of an orange crate, I've been working three years on a book that refuses to cooperate, and I'm *terrified* of women."

She replied, "Obviously, you need me. I'm young and smart and sexy and funny and talented!"

Her enthusiasm made him sad, his response to it even more so. He typed, "I'm sorry, but I am about to divorce a woman who is young and smart and funny and sexy and talented. And I have no intention of jumping out of the frying pan into the fire. I'm *tired*."

So in today's mail, finally, had arrived a picture. Nothing fancy. She wore shorts, a baggy sweater, and aerobic sneakers. The pose, on a porch railing, was mockingly cheesecake.

And it triggered an erection.

Two

Blue patches of sky appeared to the northwest and east; thunderous outbursts receded farther south. The rain let up, died away. He started hunting again, always climbing, slowly, slowly. His heart strained against the leash of all the drugs in his body, but it stayed in synch. When he felt it about to go out, he would stop and rest until everything was okay again.

He came to a grove of mature aspens whose crowns towered high above. Among their trunks rising from tall green grasses were hundreds of enormous ferns. They were a pleasant beige color—cinnamon, to be more precise. It was five-thirty, and although sunlight created a warm yellow fire high in the aspen crowns, down below the light was melancholy, yet radiant, as if lit not by natural causes but by a human mood.

Weather held its breath: no wind, no forest noises. He floated through the glen. The high wet grass and the fern leaves swiped at his hips, soaking them. He stepped on spongy moss, climbed over a massive downed trunk, and headed up another road. It was as much fun to check out all these different roads as it was to journey from one pool to another on the big river while fishing. Around every bend, always, lay something different.

He hated leaving behind that lovely grove. It would have been nice to share the mood with somebody . . . like the girl who would arrive in three days? In this morning's epistle, as in so many others, she had praised his rage and sexuality. She recounted in too, too vivid detail dreams about him and herself in compromising positions. Poor baby. If only she knew how barren his sex life had been the last two years. The old days, the profligate days, were over.

How could anyone, let alone a person that young, be so aggressive with a total stranger?

In his entire life he had never written a single fan letter. Nor made the first move with a woman.

Eventually, the road petered out. He headed up the canyon in a southeasterly direction on a deer and sheep trail. The entire hillside, a southern exposure and in shadow, was populated by massive aspens growing close together. He could see bright sunshine about a quarter mile downhill, closer to the creek. The ground was almost bare, mulched by leaves, and there were very few old trees spread-eagled on the mossy ground. It was as calm and somber here as in the previous grove.

He was rejoicing in his solitude when a sheep bleated about a quarter mile uphill. Crestfallen, he turned south, left the trail, and traversed down the steep slope to a lower road beside the creek. He didn't want to meet the herder, another human being. Sometimes, yes, he liked chatting in Spanish. Invariably, the herders were from Mexico and enjoyed talking to an oddball gringo in the middle of nowhere.

Until about two years ago, he'd often driven into these mountains with an aged friend. The old man had been raised herding sheep and shearing them, and he liked to visit the valley's few remaining flocks. During the springtime hijadero they went to sheep camps across the river on the mesa and watched the lambing and shearing. From July through September they visited animals grazing the high country on Forest Service permits. The old man enjoyed gossiping with herders in Spanish. Born in 1898, he had lived a rural life of quiet integrity. When he and the writer hooked up twenty years ago, they became good friends and political allies. In retirement, the old man was an important spokesman for the valley. He led many struggles for land and water rights and testified often down in the legislature on behalf of farmers, small ranchers, the dispossessed. The younger man had written his speeches, done research, attended a thousand meetings.

At ninety, the old man slowed down, lost his driver's license. His wife died. He had prostate cancer and no family within three hundred miles to care for him. So for three years the younger man came every day to the small trailer to talk, deliver shopping and medicines, prepare meals. The old man became legally blind from macular degeneration, so the writer read aloud to him many books, including the autobiography of Reies Tijerina in Spanish. They loved each other without fanfare. When the old man died in December a year ago, the younger man had lost a friend closer to himself, almost, than any member of his own immediate family.

Around six-thirty, while walking a grassy road on a north slope south of the creek, he came to a bend that held a seepage of water. The area was ankle-deep in rich green clover. He inspected the puddle, set like a gem in a frame of jade-green moss, but found only deer prints, no grouse. About twenty yards higher, however, he discovered five calcium-white bird droppings. Despite the rain, they crumbled when he pinched them, days old.

In the photograph, she wore an insouciant, enigmatic smile, hard to pin down. Was she shy underneath . . . or every bit as intimidating as her letters?

A little after seven he began his descent. Each aspen leaf on the mossy road held many droplets of rainwater. An odd luminescent light floating down through the trees ahead made it seem as if he were descending a path decorated by tiny clusters of diamonds. He halted for a couple of minutes in order to appreciate the scene. Then he forged ahead in more of a hurry, eager to be out before dark.

* * *

At the truck, during the last moments of twilight, he mixed a vodka and Diet Coke and listened to an owl hooting about fifty yards downhill along the creek bed. It went *hoot-a-loo*, *a-who*, *who*, repeated many times. He called softly once or twice, mimicking the noise, and remembered when he had been camped in a grove of tall spruces up in Garcia Park with his children, and an owl had been perched in the nearest tree. He had talked to it for almost half an hour while lying on a mattress in the bed of his truck with a child in either arm. Maybe fifteen years ago. That would have made the boy eight, the girl four. He could smell an odor from their campfire long ago.

The ice rattled a little in his glass. He talked to the owl, and the owl talked back. Their conversation went on like that for a while.

Later, he parked at the edge of the road about fifty feet above his favorite beaver ponds. The water was clear and absolutely tranquil except for the trout. The reflection of yellow willow leaves rippled in circles whenever a fish dimpled the surface. They were feeding casually, in no hurry, almost satiated. Pines beyond the willows were dark, nearly black. He lifted his eyes to the conifer silhouette along the ridge of the canyon. A quarter moon shone brightly above the jagged tips of the trees.

Then—finally—he slipped her picture from the envelope on his dash and gazed at it for a long time in the dying light, and he gave in completely to the excitement.

Three

They sat down across from each other in a quiet café. She was slightly chubby, dark-haired, wore glasses. She was nervous and spoke too quickly, and he had a hard time following. She wore a striped jersey, shorts, white socks, and aerobic sneakers. So as not to seem self-conscious or hypocritical, he wore his usual attire, a faded shirt and dirty pants and sloppy sneakers. What you see is what you get. Her eyes were very dark and bright. Her upper lip trembled because she was nervous. Of all the ways to describe her, this one struck him first: *She's young.* And immediately her youth caused an ache all out of proportion.

But he was in beyond his depth, and of course it was completely out of kilter and unbalanced **right from the start.**

Despite all the bold rhetoric and intimate revelations of her letters, she was a total stranger. He couldn't remember a single fact about her life.

About him she said in awe:

"This is unbelievable, it's totally weird."

"What is?"

"Well, for months I've had a yearning for you, we've exchanged bunches of raunchy letters, and then, well, here I am, and there you are. Like, *plop.*"

"I'm a disappointment?"

"I don't know. Your voice sounds funny. You . . . you're *real.*"

"That's bad?"

"No. But real is weird. I can't control you like I did in my head. Every time you open your mouth, a different clown jumps out. It's like suddenly meeting a . . . movie star!"

Her amazement was so completely without artifice that instantly he fell in love.

Of course, he fell right out again when she said, "You look *old,*" and then immediately compounded her mistake by adding, "And you look like a bum, too."

He shrugged. "Fortunately, how I look is my own business."

"**Are you trying to pretend that you're not** rich and famous?"

"I am not rich and famous."

Her eyes flashed at the challenge. Suddenly, she was like a cat, and he was the ball at the end of a swinging string. Insufferably brazen, she reached out and batted the ball.

"I despise hypocrites."

He sighed. Was all youth so black and white? He didn't have the energy anymore.

They talked about various things: her background, his background. He caught himself a couple of times beginning a sentence, "When I was your age—"

She cut that off pronto. "Don't you pull rank on me."

"I am not pulling rank. I only—"

"You're a chauvinist," she said in triumph. "In your books you pretend not to be. But in reality you are. Are you racist also?"

He looked at his watch and said, "I'm sorry, but your twenty minutes of browbeating are up."

She smiled, vindictive, victorious. "Patronizing also. I knew it. What a disappointment. For your information, you don't interest me at all."

"You wrote all those letters."

"*You* answered them."

Her eyes were positively gleaming.

But soon enough the wind changed. Obviously worried at this rocky start, she sought to make amends.

"I'm sorry, but I'm so nervous I could die. I mean, we wrote so much stuff to each other in letters, and now it's like we're not even real people, or something. Would it be okay if I kiss you?"

Grateful for her impudence and valor, he leaned forward and brushed his lips against her mouth. Her body shivered. She poked her tonguetip against his two front teeth (which were false). He smiled; then she smiled and pulled back, her cheeks colored bright crimson.

"Whew." She assessed him in astonishment. "I'm glad *that's* done. Boy, have I ever been jonesing for you."

Then she placed one palm against her chest and giggled nervously.

"I think I'm gonna have a cow."

But in the very next minute she asked if they could leave. "I can't talk anymore. I think we better make love and get it over with."

He nodded. "Come to my apartment. It isn't far." Trying to be lighthearted, he added, "If we both lie down sideways, there'll be enough room."

Truth is, it wasn't all that much fun to be fifty years old, a "noted" author, nearly broke, and living in a space smaller than his first New York apartment, which had been a sixth-floor walkup on the corner of Prince and West Broadway that had rented for forty-two fifty a month nearly thirty years ago.

She'd rather they went to her room. "It's neutral. Nobody we know ever made love with either of us in it before."

Four

It was a nice old room with a small adobe fireplace, a polished wooden floor, a high ceiling and massive vigas, and a wide window looking out on cottonwoods framing a small hayfield bordered by plum thickets. There was a floor lamp, a simple wooden table, a single bed, a refrigerator, sink, and an antique gas stove. Her purple sleeping bag lay crumpled on the bed. Her typewriter and a ream of paper sat on the table. A music stand and a violin case occupied one corner. She had brought a few books and arranged them along the windowsill. He inspected them, of course: *Love in the Time of Cholera*; Antonio Skármeta's *Burning Patience*; Pablo Neruda's *Veinte Poemas de Amor*. Also two of his own works: a brutal novel about violence in American culture, and a lyrical nonfiction hosanna to life on the deserted mesa west of town.

Then he stood there totally lost, with no idea how to begin.

"What's the matter?" she asked.

"I'm scared," he admitted.

"Me too."

She cleared a Walkman and some tapes off the sleeping bag. They kissed standing up. He held her tightly to stop the trembling. Then they were on the bed, fumbling, uncomfortable, pressing too hard, totally out of rhythm. He had no idea how to implement such sudden sex. This might qualify as the most self-conscious moment of his life.

Terrified of AIDS, he had brought a condom. But when the time came, she said, "I hate rubbers—don't you dare."

"It's crazy not to."

"Please . . ." She kissed hungrily. "Mellow out. Stop being an old fogy."

He knew it was foolish, but complied.

Then all at once they clicked. All at once he pushed inside and she gave a little cry and her eyes glazed, and for a moment it seemed he would never stop sinking into her and he almost cried out in surprise, pain, and relief. An incredible rush weakened his body.

He asked, "What do you use for birth control?"

"Nothing."

The excitement doubled.

At the last second he withdrew and came against her thigh. She ordered him to go down on her so she could climax also. He obeyed. She gripped his hair, guiding urgently. It was a great strain for her, and his jaws ached, but they made it happen. She coughed and flinched into a fetal position, whimpering.

When he touched her neck she huddled up in a ball against him so that he could envelop all of her in his arms. They stayed that way without moving for a long time. From where his head lay he could look out the window at prisms of light dancing in ripples of foliage.

He was amazed that this could happen. He was astonished by her audacity. It didn't seem real. At her age he'd been a virgin, and a simple kiss would have sent him to seventh heaven.

She whispered, "I love you. I love you with all my heart. That was incredible."

He was so grateful that he almost said "I love you" back, but then caught himself just in the nick of time.

Quietly holding the girl, he remembered something that happened with his first wife when she was only twenty and he was twenty-three, and they had been married for seven days. They were in a small white room in their new Manhattan apartment, making love on a mattress on the floor. There was no other furniture in the room; their discarded clothes lay in a corner. His wife had a silver bracelet on her left wrist. She was tanned but for the white outlines created on her skin by a bikini. Through a large open window fresh spring breezes entered, tickling their damp flesh. You could hear children on the playground of St. Anthony's parish school. They made love like innocent babes. Sweet it was, and not particularly erotic.

All at once a colorful bird flew through the window and panicked, fluttering against the recently painted white walls, unable to escape. He and his wife jumped up and tried to help. The bird was a male Baltimore oriole. At first they tried to guide it in flight toward the open window, but for some reason it kept fleeing in the wrong directions. Feathers floated onto the mattress. So they changed tactics and tried to capture the frightened oriole. And at the end of a hectic and awkward pursuit, she snagged the bird, hurried over to the window, and set it free.

Five

Next day she was feeling cocky and obnoxious. "Teach me to hunt. I want to kill harmless little animals."

"Please, I hunt alone."

"I want to fuck you and then kill things and then fuck you again."

"Don't be so melodramatic."

She folded her arms, slumped forward, and clammed up.

He relented. "Why do you really want to hunt?"

"Oh for God's sake, don't be so dense. I'm being sarcastic."

He observed her while she stewed, perhaps the most erotic woman he'd ever met. Correction: the situation and the age difference made her so. A criminal liaison. Her sloppy blouse drifted off one shoulder, and he was mesmerized by the soft line of her collarbone. She had full, pouty lips, always atremble from the intensity of her anger, nerves, insecurity . . . *feelings*.

"Hunting is sort of . . ."—he hesitated, but couldn't think of a better word—"sacred to me." He was embarrassed and apologetic. "Sacred" was not a word he would have selected, had he been at his typewriter, with time and a thesaurus, trying.

"Oh, cut the bullshit, mon," she laughed, mocking him. " 'Sacred,' no less. You're so totally bogus."

But even while speaking she reached out to tweak his nose in a cheerfully seductive gesture.

That afternoon, as she came out and approached the truck toting her gear, he blurted, "What the hell is *that*?"

"What the hell does it *look* like?" she replied, grinning.

"It looks like your violin case."

She licked the tip of her finger and poked it

against his forehead. "Congratulations, you get a gold star."

He said, "You don't take a violin grouse hunting."

"*I* am not grouse hunting, *you* are."

After a perplexed beat, he said, "You're crazy."

She gave him a sly, challenging look. Then she reached for his right wrist and lifted his hand. She fitted his index finger in her mouth and formed a pouty O around it with her lips. Her taunting eyes directly engaged him while she sucked lightly. Then she pushed back the wrist, freeing his finger, and her mischievous little smile gave him a surprisingly erotic start.

"No I'm not," she said.

And he believed her.

To get there they had to climb. At first it was steep and moderately difficult. Young aspens and alders, head-high corn lilies and huge dying cow parsnip made the trail seem almost tropical. She held his hand for a minute while singing a Grateful Dead tune. Her voice, though young, had a faint and alluring rasp:

> *Driving that train,*
> *high on cocaine,*
> *Casey Jones, you'd better*
> *watch your speed—*

Then she broke away, gamboling ahead, so ripe in tantalizing energy that he almost cried out in delight.

Later, they zigzagged between baby spruce trees, no higher than their shoulders, growing in the road. He stopped once to point out blue gentians; again to expose the fruit on a thimbleberry; and a third time to ponder a flurry of baby bugs on the underside of an oshá leaf. Whenever they paused, she hugged him like an affectionate puppy and nibbled on one ear or another. Then she plucked the leaf or the flower and slipped it carefully between the pages of her yellow notebook after writing down its name.

It was hard on his heart. He could barely breathe and had to proceed slowly to avoid fibrillations. Soon she began to forge ahead thirty or forty yards, then wait impatiently for him to arrive. He grinned wistfully when he caught up. Sometimes she gave him a little peck on the cheek, other times she asked, "How's the old ticker?"

Invariably, he replied, "Oh, I can't complain."

Teasing, she rubbed close against him and cupped his genitals. She breathed into his ear and licked the lobe—instantly he went hard.

She laughed—"Uh oh, trouble in River City"—and pranced off, swinging around the aspens, hopping over dead logs.

It was almost like watching himself at her age, galloping away from the older person he'd become.

"Wait up," he cried in mock agony. "Don't leave me."

"No way," she sang, performing impromptu dance steps that were fetchingly self-conscious. "I'm too young to be saddled and tamed!"

She had a way of dancing on the balls of her feet when she walked, all peppy, straining at the leash. It was free-form and cocky. It seemed to him that she was always in motion, twisting, turning, forging ahead, doubling back. It could be fatiguing. Her fingers always puttered, flicking in the air, scribbling against the surface of things. She liked to touch him, but her hands never tarried. She moved away, came back, her knuckles brushed wisplike against his chest or shoulders. When talking, she had an absent-minded habit of touching his butt or gently hitting his shoulder for emphasis. But the second she merged against him, she was gone. He would have liked to hold her still, but she could not stand to be trapped like that. Her energy was exalting and arrogant and irrepressible. Yes, she reminded him of himself at that age . . . and for many years after. Used to be he had driven people crazy with his manic style. Now turnabout was fair play, qué no?

She scribbled fingers in the air, playing a flamenco guitar.

Invisible and inaudible musical notes clustered about her like a merry flock of bees, and **he laughed, and she laughed in return.**

Suddenly, she whirled around hanging on to a sapling and balanced on tiptoes, laughing. A butterfly flip-flapped between them. She stuck out her tongue and gave a tantalizing wiggle of her hips. When he reached her, they kissed, but only for an instant: *ping!*—then gone.

"I'm tired," he said. "I need a little break."

So they sat in the grass eating apples. A red squirrel chattered. A tall tree was creaking like a mast under the weight of old-fashioned rigging. A minuscule wren on a log made a faint sound: *chirrr, chirrr*. She fiddled on the ground, picking up small white snail shells. He followed the progress of a slender, incarnadine insect clawing among the fluffy white tendrils of a salsify seed head, which resembled a gigantic dandelion.

Six

"I didn't *believe* you would ever write me back," she said. "I figured it wasn't even a one-in-a-billion chance. And then when the letter arrived and I saw the return address—wow! I almost fainted—I really did. What a coup! I must've read that letter over a hundred times. I was walking around on air, in a daze, really. You know what I kept doing? I kept lifting my hand up and kissing the back of it, pretending it was you. I would give my hand these incredible heartfelt kisses. I lay in bed night after night so excited I couldn't sleep. I placed my palm against my lips and gave you the most merciful kisses that ever happened in the history of humankind. Of course, every night I also made up scenarios of us together and I masturbated. It wasn't what you might think, though—my fantasies. We never made love. We would be walking someplace hand in hand, wearing old sweaters and kicking up autumn leaves. I had this, like, *totally* psycho happiness I can't explain. We never took our clothes off, but Jesus, my *feeling* for you was tremendous. I was levitating above the bed, it was so powerful."

"That's pretty hard to live up to," he said with a rueful smile. "Reality must be a letdown."

"When the real you walked into the café I almost died. I don't know how words came out of my mouth. Inside, I was paralyzed."

"You didn't seem that way."

"I've never been that shaken in my life."

He admitted, "Me too."

She revealed, "When I'm scared I act pretty obnoxious. I'm sorry."

"It's okay."

They squeezed each other. It popped into his head: *I could have a child with this woman.*

Then it popped out of his head at the speed of light.

Seven

"Jesus!"

A grouse flushed out of the spruce tree with a shocking clatter of wings. It headed downhill past them through aspens at what seemed like a hundred miles an hour. His first snapshot kicked loose tail feathers; the second disemboweled the bird and it crumpled, bouncing off white tree trunks on its way to the ground.

She had dropped to all fours and was squatting, hands over her ears, astonished and mortified. She did not move while he went over and picked up the bloody bundle. The bird was ruined because he had shot it at close range.

"God, that happened so *fast*," she exclaimed.

"It always does."

"It scared the living daylights out of me."

"Me too. Never fails."

"That was an incredible shot. I'm impressed. I don't *believe* your quick reactions."

"Usually, I miss. I'm not very good."

Her eyes changed in a wink, going frosty. "If there's one thing I hate, it's false humility. Phony modesty."

He laughed and told her, "You'll see."

"Of course. Now, just to prove you're always right, you'll deliberately miss on purpose."

He faced away from her and bit his tongue. Her abrupt swings in mood were disconcerting. Given half a chance, most of his life, he'd always walked a mile out of his way to avoid confrontations.

A confused deer wandered into the clearing, stopped, pricked its enormous ears, took their measure, then skipped sideways and vanished.

"Have you ever killed a deer?"

"No."

"Why not?"

"I don't know. Too big, maybe."

"You kill fish and doves and grouse—why not deer?"

"Not deer, not bear, not bobcats, not mountain lion, not elk."

"Do you get off on being so righteous about that moral position? Choosing what to kill, what not to? I bet you don't screw married women either. What makes a grouse less sacred than a deer? Do you get off on playing God?"

"Not at all."

"A fish is no different from a mountain lion," she said. "It's a living thing."

In a gesture of truce, he placed his hand across her breasts.

With a toss of her head she shook him off.

Then she finally realized. "Yuk, what did you *do* to that bird?"

"It was too close. The pattern hadn't begun to spread."

She lifted her shirt and ordered him to paint her tits with his bloody fingers. Afterwards, when he knelt at the puddle of a nearby spring and washed his hands, the water was so cold it made his wrists hurt. They tingled for almost fifteen minutes.

She nuzzled under his chin and slipped her hand into his trousers. "Actually, that was pretty groovy, dude. It happened so fast and sudden and noisy. You killed it without thinking, death was so *quick*. I hate to admit this, but it's kind of a turn-on. You're a cold-blooded bastard, aren't you?"

"I don't think so."

"Oh damn you." She pulled away. "Don't you have even *one* honest response in your body? Tell me the *truth*."

He cast his eyes to the ground, frustrated, sad, fatigued. Truth? *Which* truth? His estranged wife had always demanded it from him, and he had always tried, but his truth was never the truth she wanted. She asked him once about a past lover, a woman from New Jersey. "Was she a heavy flame? Did you love her?" He had thought carefully and replied, no, it had never been a question of love, but they were longtime friends. There had been little passion in their lovemaking, nothing truly erotic. But they had cared for each other. They only made love—and he counted exactly—seven times. His wife folded her arms and taunted, "I don't believe a word you say. You wouldn't tell me the truth at gunpoint, and frankly, knowing me, I don't blame you."

Many times, in response to her probing, he had bared his soul, answering intimate questions with what he considered to be total candor. But always she found a way to accuse him of false-hood. Either that, or everything he revealed on request was later used as ammunition against him. Or it made her jealous, defensive, angry.

Finally he shut up and quit digging that hole any deeper.

The truth was he did not think of himself as cold-blooded. The truth was he felt compassion toward almost everybody and everything. The truth was that he hunted carefully, and had spent much of his life working on behalf of the environment, wildlife habitat, the wretched of the earth. He had contradictions, certainly, but never thought of himself as cruel. Of course, anyone can make a case for anything against anybody. To defend yourself is usually taken as an admission of guilt.

So he let her comments ride.

Toward evening, he rested on a log and had a sip of water, then bit into an apple. She clicked open the violin case and removed her instrument and a bow. She twisted the adjusting nut to tighten up the horsehair, then rubbed a piece of rosin against the filaments.

Walking off a ways, she said, "At least one of us should apologize to the forest gods for killing that poor critter." Then she began to play. The piercing blues tune caught him completely by surprise. It had never occurred to him that she might be *good*. The violin had never been mentioned in any of her letters. And yet the notes she produced were absolutely clean and controlled and they bent off the strings with a heartrending emotional clairvoyance.

She dipped and weaved a little, but nothing flamboyant, nothing to call attention. The moment her bow had started to shape that first note, she became a professional.

She played a melody not of this world. It was haunting, imbued with a melancholy ache, a bit slurred, like the voice of Billie Holiday. He shook his head, unable to comprehend how this girl in glasses, a sloppy sweatshirt, nondescript shorts, and fancy aerobic sneakers could produce such an incongruous yet wonderful moment.

When she stopped, he asked, "What was that?"

She came over, squatted in front of him, gave a daffy and self-conscious smile, then leaned forward and licked the tip of his nose.

"I call it 'Blues for a Decent Guy.' "

He said, "Oh."

Almost plaintively, she wondered, "Do you think I'll be able to love the real you as much as I loved the paper person?"

Eight

When he took a first draft of the divorce papers over to the house, his wife asked him to climb up in their small tree and hand apples down to her. He went halfway to the top before the limbs became too fragile to bear his weight. She stood on the penultimate rung of a ladder and raised her open hand to him. He placed in her palm a ripe fruit. The yellowing leaves were almost obliterated by shiny crimson globes. This was the best year in a decade. Branches were bent and weary from carrying so much weight.

He said, "Each time I pluck one, the branch says, 'Thank you.' "

He picked quickly, clasping the wonderful fruits, pinching leaves off the stem as he blindly extended his arm down behind his buttocks, transferring the apple to her hand. She placed each one carefully in her sack. They were a precision team. He leaned out, holding on with one hand, stretching up to pick with the other.

"We'll leave the tip-toppers for the birds."

She agreed.

About every forty apples he stopped. She descended the ladder and walked through waist-high grass in the small orchard to the edge of the garden, where a wheelbarrow stood between hills of squash whose leaves had recently been blackened by the first frost. Rotten crab apples from the neighboring tree were squashed in the tousled brome. Carefully, she emptied her sack, piling apples into the wheelbarrow. She seemed sad and beautiful, near tears. She returned with a languid, melancholy air through the grass and climbed the ladder back up to him.

He handed down apples, reaching on tiptoes as high as he could to filch a handful of final beauties. The rest he left to the birds. She retreated down and walked away. He stayed in the crown of the tree, watching her.

* * *

His wife put a narrow mattress on the floor between the cartons of apples. The odor cleaved like a wondrous malignancy—evocative, provocative. Apples, clean and crisp and cidery. She lit a candle. He picked a few sprigs of sage and placed them in a bottle, sprinkled on some water, and set the bottle beside the candle among the laden boxes. It was too cold to remove their clothes. She rolled onto her stomach and barely pushed her old jeans down below her buttocks. He wedged a pillow under her belly to raise the rump. Head sideways, pressed against the striped ticking, she stared at the candle flame and inhaled the tang of apples.

Under the floorboards skunks were scratching. He crushed sage leaves in his fingers, then mingled in her juices and painted the hollow of her throat with this elixir: sage, apple, woman.

She lay quiet and passive, letting her orgasm happen on its own instead of rushing to it. His moves were considerate, almost shy—they rarely made love anymore and lacked familiarity. To her it had no meaning without "commitment." As for him?—he luxuriated in sensations and ignored the bigger picture. The woman existed as catalyst; his entire body was penis.

Yet she had a strong climax in spite of herself. At the center of it she began weeping. He teased himself to the edge, holding it until long after she had subsided. When finally he released semen, there came to his heart an amazing roar of sensation.

The atmosphere changed when they spoke about the divorce. He had typed up a new agreement, determined to avoid lawyers. He had his first and her second divorce papers for examples, and the process seemed straightforward so long as they agreed. At first, he'd wanted to draw a line through the property, saving himself the back field. But the zoning laws prohibited subdividing with rights to build unless he was granted a variance by the Planning Commission. To have it resurveyed would cost a mint. There would have to be new title insurance, an updated abstract, and a dozen other nitpicking legal maneuvers, all of which seemed superfluous and costly. Then, deciding it would be dumb for them to be neighbors anyway, he let go of the land and little house (even though it was legally his separate property), whereupon everything became quite simple.

Except, of course, she did not want a divorce. "I still love you, and I want it to work. Everybody in town is rooting for us." When he'd finally left home a year ago, in bad shape, out of love, ready to call it quits, he had wanted to keep it friendly. However, that seemed impossible. Bottom line, she believed in all or nothing. "I'm not going to be just another one of your lovers. I think it's obscene, all the incest in this town. Everybody's ex-wives and -husbands and -lovers are so sophisticated and polite to each other. Well, not me. I am a passionate woman, and I know how to hate. You made a commitment, and now you refuse to honor it. I despise this discard society. You promised to stand by me in all kinds of emotional weather, and now you don't even respect me enough to see a shrink. You have betrayed me and I won't forgive you."

They had been married exactly five years.

She withdrew after their lovemaking, as if he'd bamboozled her into sex against her wishes. They had come together only a dozen times during the past year. She was cold and aloof as their bodies cooled. Though he wanted to run away, he gave her the papers to read, including a Waiver of Appearance and Trial form to be signed and notarized.

"I think you are a terrible man." She looked him straight in the eye. "When this thing is over I will never speak to you again."

He repressed all his anger, all his bitterness, everything, every emotion. Twenty years ago he had planted four aspen saplings on the other side of the woodpile near the southwest corner of the garden. The trees had been a gift from a dear friend who subsequently committed suicide. Now the trees had reached a height of almost thirty feet, and their leaves were turning yellow.

On his way out, he took a hard look at everything. The half-acre back field with the four elm trees at the far end and the raggedy barbwire fence he'd kept patching with baling wire for twenty years. The slab sheds he'd built twenty years ago with his four-year-old son while his first wife had been in Cuba on a Venceremos brigade. He remembered how for several years they'd raised chickens, geese, guinea hens, turkeys. They milked two goats. The kids rode a couple of Shetland ponies. There had been dogs, several cats . . . and later on his boy had kept fancy pigeons in the chicken coop.

Then his eyes flicked over the garden area, which he had tilled without interruption since 1969. And the big old crab apple tree, the two regular apple trees, the handful of small pear trees, and the greengage plums. Next, the woodpile: for two decades he had brought slash back from the forest, building an enormous pile. He chopped all winter, feeding three stoves. Behind the woodpile stood the outhouse he both loved and hated, and beside it the toolshed his daughter had helped to build ten years ago. The roof over his tiny one-room office was another of his masterful carpentry jobs: warped, tilting,

somewhat skewed, it nevertheless kept out the
water. It made him smile, that roof. As a car-
penter he was a total neophyte, a screwball. He
specialized in a style called "building boxes."
Crude, but serviceable. Roofs and sheds. (By
appointment only!)

Beside the house were rosebushes and some
hollyhocks, which had been there long before
his new wife arrived to start landscaping. And
the big apricot tree he'd planted as a seedling.

Grackles were gathered on bird feeders he'd
nailed to fence posts in front of the kitchen window, just above the irrigation ditch. He had
loved the grackles on those feeders; them and
the starlings and blackbirds, and the migrating
grosbeaks in spring and autumn. Silver-tipped
poplars and honey locusts grew along the ditch
bank. Then came the half-acre front field in
which grazed his neighbor's old swaybacked
mare. She had used that field for eleven years,
always free, a goodwill gesture.

By the time he reached the paved road and
cast a final glance up at a dying cottonwood in
which Lewis's woodpeckers or flickers nested
each spring, he was grinding his teeth in a rage,
and felt like crying.

Nine

He loved calling her attention to things.

Under dead aspen trees lying across their path
were piles of fresh sawdust caused by hungry
bugs excavating beneath the blackened bark. At
the seeps he could usually find deer tracks. He
never missed a feather on the ground; of a
flicker, a junco, a Steller's jay. A ruptured stump
had probably been torn apart by a bear hungry
for ants. Aspen saplings had been broken about
chest-high by deer cleaning their antlers.

He identified butterflies: alpines, an angle-
wing, two fritillaries. And birds: more specifi-

cally, right this moment, a flock of siskins pecking at yellow thistles. He could have observed for hours as they sent a fusillade of feathery tufts drifting across the narrow canyon into evergreen branches above the creek.

When he tarried at a clump of delicate white mushrooms half submerged in tall green grass, she asked, "Are they poisonous?"

"I don't know."

She nudged her toe forward and casually rent them asunder.

"They don't *look* poisonous."

He envied her casual annihilations. He would have enjoyed some freedom from the weight of his conscience. It might have been exhilarating to participate in the voluptuous trashing of life.

During a break, she told him about one of her boyfriends. They had lived together for about six months. He was tall and thin, with a mustache—an architecture student. Since his parents were loaded, he drove a BMW. He was a great tennis player, and a pretty good amateur pianist, too. They were both into drugs, and after a while things got sort of squirrelly. She couldn't stand marijuana but liked cocaine. He started cheating on her with her supposedly best friend. So she went and fucked one of *his* bosom buddies. It accelerated like that until finally they were arguing all the time. The sexual infidelities became downright sloppy. Finally, she quit doing drugs and kicked him out. "He was all fucked up and flunking out of school by then." She felt suicidal. The fast lane had been a kick for a minute, but it sure disintegrated quickly.

"I never wanted it, either," she explained. "I loved him. I still do. He's a special person, like you. I remember one day, in the middle of all the bullshit, I was at home alone in the apartment, just cleaning up and setting things to order before he returned. Sun streamed through the windows. My cat, Misha, was curled up in a ball snoozing on the couch. There was a classical tape on the stereo, something like Chopin piano preludes or a little Mozart. Stew was bubbling on the stove. I actually even had an ironing board out, and was pressing a few of his shirts. He liked clean shirts and dressed very sharp. And at that moment I was nearly crushed by a fist of happiness, I almost started crying. I thought, This is what I really want in my life: a little home and a man I love and my cat asleep on the couch. All the rest of it, all the craziness and excitement, is so totally bogus."

Then she was staring at him with a lewd lack of constraint. Her saucy tonguetip filched a crumb of chocolate off her bottom lip. She lowered her eyelids halfway and smirked. She was a devil, bewitching, nasty, coy. And hungry. He gazed back at her from the plateau of being fifty, both puzzled and excited.

"What are you thinking?" she asked slyly, shifting her rump, raising one leg, and dawdling it over his knee.

"What do you think, idiot?"

"I am not an idiot," she announced primly, eyes instantly hostile, causing his heart to lurch.

"I didn't mean—" he began to explain, but her hand crept over and clasped his fingers, shushing.

"Relax, I'm not going to bite you."

"I never know."

"Don't wear a rubber," she whispered.

"I should. It's stupid not to. We need to be safe. . . ."

She pouted. "I *hate* safe."

"Me too."

"You're such a dork."

She laughed softly and kissed him.

After they made love, she told him a story about the book she wanted to write. It would only have three main characters: an older man, a younger woman, and a little child, a girl named Maria, who would be about six. The man was an ex-ballplayer who had turned to gambling and drink. The young woman, his daughter, was a hooker who'd given up the streets to take care of her dad, who was dying of Lou Gehrig's disease. Maria, a beautiful angelic girl, was the result of an accident one night on the hustings—so her father was an unknown john. Maria's mother and granddad had taught the little girl to walk a tightrope high above the ground. While she balanced up there dressed in pink tights and a lemon-yellow tutu, she played a ukulele and sang "It's a Sin to Tell a Lie."

This trio traveled all over the United States putting on their show in plazas and ballparks, vacant lots and hockey rinks. Maria was like a slave or a dancing bear. She hated being a silly little girl playing a ukulele on a high wire. So one night she escaped and wound up living on a farm in Kansas with a man and a woman who raised cantaloupes and were deaf-mutes.

"Then what happens?" he nudged, after a long pause.

She shook her head. "I don't know. But something will happen. It always does when you write, doesn't it? I never know what's gonna happen next. I love it. When you're writing, every page is an adventure."

He envied her, but refrained from comment. And they hiked out of the mountains in the dark, occasionally bumping against each other.

Ten

He worked at night, and she did also. They sat
in separate rooms about a mile apart at two in
the morning, typing away: *tap tap tappety tap tap*.
He pictured her able to sit still concentrating for
an hour or two hours or longer, banging on the
keys, piling up pages and pages of words. Perhaps she jiggled her feet as she typed, dancing
out the rhythms. On the other hand, he moved
slowly. He wrote paragraphs by hand on scrap
paper, and read them over twenty times, cor-
recting, before transferring them to the type-
written page. He got up often and nibbled on a

carrot, or had a shot of juice. Writing and despair went hand in hand. He finished a page, then clicked through TV channels, just grazing. For years the routine had rarely varied. "Never hesitate to procrastinate." He had four or five books by other authors in progress, picked one up, read a few pages, but could not concentrate, lost interest. He returned to the desk, perused what he'd written, stood up again. He went out to the middle of his tiny lawn and gazed at the stars. The town was awful quiet.

After a minute he lifted his hand and tenderly kissed each knuckle.

Tap . . . tap . . . tappety . . . tap . . . tap.

Eleven

First he mixed a drink. Then he took the fishing
vest and a sewing kit out of his apartment to
the round wooden table with the jumble of
bones on it: deer antlers, horse jawbones, a coyote skull, delicate ribs, and the six-month-old
carcass of a magpie he'd found in the gutter
while riding his bike. He pushed the bones aside
to make room, then crossed the lawn and
plucked an apple from the small, heavily laden
tree. Though mostly green, the apple had a few
pink shadings. It was hard yet not too bitter.
He liked the tartness, which puckered his

cheeks. The wild taste mixed well with his drink.

He sat down and emptied all the vest pockets: his fishing doodads, gewgaws, gimcracks. They made a busy little pile on the table. Six fly boxes of differing sizes and compartmentalization, a dozen commercial nine-foot leaders, a Sucrets tin holding spinners: Mepps, two Colorados, some Panther Martins. There were Band-Aids and matches, a film canister of swivels, two plastic sacks of 3/0 lead split shot, a tiny Phillips screwdriver for tightening up reels, a Swiss Army knife, which needed to be cleaned and oiled, half a dozen spools of Berkeley leader material in the ten-, eight-, and six-pound categories, also a packet of size 8 snelled hooks, and another package of gold salmon egg hooks with which he caught chubs to use as bait when the river was muddy.

He took needle and thread and repaired several tears in the vest. Then he emptied the fly boxes, pried all leader knot material off the eyelets of previously cast flies, and made piles of the flies he most favored. Small brown and black ones, many Peacock Nymphs and Gold Ribbed Hare's Ears, a profusion of Wooly-Boogers, and simple black size 10 Wooly Worms. He was also partial to Spruce Flies and Spruce Matuka Streamers, Muddler Minnows, and a bucktail with real jungle cock feathers to show it had been purchased years ago.

He replenished two boxes with flies he used

most often and put away the others as "extras." Then he opened every blade in the Swiss Army knife and with toothpicks painstakingly cleaned out the grit inside each blade chamber. He oiled the springs, wiggled blades to make sure oil was sinking in, and wiped everything clean.

He paused, taking a bite of apple, and sipped on his drink. The sky was cloudy, fretful, interesting. He chewed reflectively while sewing the torn flap of his vest's zipper back into the nap. He worked slowly and clumsily, but it was thick thread and would hold well, he surmised, provided he employed enough stitches.

Next, he removed a spool of 7-weight double-tapered floating line from his large Pflueger reel and meticulously cleaned grains of sand from the reel mechanism. He applied graphite lubricating grease to the spindle, oiled the drag screw and the ratchet bearing, replaced the spool, and tightened all the plate screws.

His drink was finished; he sucked on a cube of ice. He had worked for an hour and twenty minutes performing these small tasks, loving every moment. It gave him great pleasure to put things in order, carefully maintaining the equipment.

If only he could organize his life as brilliantly.

The tinkering had put him in a lazy, pleasantly woozy mood. Eyes closed, he leaned back in his chair and folded his arms to keep his chest warm. He inhaled the odors of evening. Yesterday, the grass next door had been mowed. He could smell the oil on his knife, its traces on his fingers. The apple scent was strongest. And as dark approached and the sky became totally overcast, he smelled rain in the offing.

It grew chilly, but he tarried a moment longer, enthralled by his blindness, the wind against his cheeks, the smells around him, the rustle of nervous leaves. A raindrop hit his forehead; another splashed against his throat. He smiled, thinking: *This moment is perfect.*

Though raindrops began to fall in earnest, it took a while for them to nudge him from the pleasant lethargy. But finally they began to sting, so he roused himself and carried his precious things inside.

As serene as deep blue light, the melancholy held him. He lay half-asleep and listened to the rain. Out there big yellow leaves were everywhere on the roads, piled along the gutters, floating in puddles. There hadn't been a sun for two days. Magpies sat on fence posts, bedraggled, uneventful: for once they were not squawking. It was already snowing at higher elevations. The lawn was covered by lemon-yellow leaves. Large red apples hung in the tree outside his window. The eaves dripped soporifically. He lay on his mattress, unable to move, suspended between sleep and wakefulness, drowsily listening to the damp noises outside. Smells came in through the window; rotting leaves, manure, grasses. He wished never to waken, and drifted in and out of luxurious and slightly erotic dreams that were gone from his memory as soon as they happened. It was a beautiful and lonely morning approaching the third week of September. Distant automobiles thrummed in passing; he heard their tires sizzling. He wanted to wake up, but was drugged, down for the count. Lazily, he fondled a hard-on; his body was woozy from happiness. He ached peacefully and had no energy for masturbation. The serenity muted everything.

Then he heard a slight tapping, a rustle, and her shadow fell over the bed. She settled down and took him into her arms. She ran her tongue lightly against his lips and whispered, "What are you thinking about?"

"My old friend who died last December. I miss him."

She touched him with an almost delicate concern. "I'm sorry."

"No, no. His life was wonderful. . . ."

Twelve

It was late in the afternoon on a cold but sunny December day. Thin sunlight came through a little window in the room at the back of the trailer. The old man was lying the same way as always under the electric blanket with the bulge at his feet where the blanket cradle kept the weight of the covers off his painfully swollen ankles. The scruffy black-and-white cat snuggled against his rib cage; the Persian kitty formed a ball at the side of his neck. He was calm, breathing lightly. He had a rare serenity, and almost never complained of his aches and pains from the spreading cancer. He believed that everything was God's will, and had no fear of dying. They talked for a while, about the weather, chopping wood, how the cabañuelas calculations in January could predict the weather for an entire year. Then the old man listened as psalms were read to him in Spanish. He closed his eyes and smiled and folded his hands on his chest. He seemed to go to sleep. There was a pause of absolute quiet in the room. The younger man leaned forward to see if the chest was still moving. Then he realized that his long-time friend was held to life by only a flimsy thread. He opened the Bible again and at random read more psalms in Spanish. Though he had long feared the moment, when it arrived he was very calm. He liked the sound of his voice, the snoozing cats, the old arthritic hands clasped in peaceful resignation. The Spanish had a rhythm like poetry. There were longer pauses in his aged friend's breathing. . . .

"That's how it happened," he said. "I read him into the promised land. I never knew exactly when he died. At one point he opened his eyes and looked at me, and there was a twinkle in them. He smiled and said what he always said, when, daily, after every visit, I put drops in his aching eyes: 'Ay, que tino de borracho.' I guess those were his last words. Even after I realized he was dead, I kept reading the psalms in Spanish. He had loved them very much. I had been reading to him for three years, almost daily. Finally, I stopped and just sat there, listening to the void. Both cats were purring. His body must have felt warm to them for a long time after because of the electric blanket."

"Did you cry?"

"No, nothing. I was relieved. It was very peaceful. His eyes were shut, but his mouth was wide open. I remembered how we used to collect wood together, and he would swing a two-bladed ax all afternoon, at eighty-five years, without growing tired. He almost never took a sip of water. He remembered when there weren't any fences and you could drive a flock of sheep hundreds of miles west to Navajoland without encountering private property, barbwire, or other impediments. I had long enjoyed that space—vicariously—through knowing him."

They buried his old man in a small camposanto up against the foothills. About a foot of fresh snow lay on the ground and powdered the branches of piñon trees at the edge of the cemetery. It was a cold day, clear and sharp as a blade, very sunny and without a breath of wind. After the service the ushers took off their carnations and placed them on the coffin as it was lowered on the green nylon straps. About ten of them stayed afterwards to fill in the grave. Shovels were brought from a couple of pickups and passed around. People took turns with the palas, heaping dirt onto the coffin. A couple of old boys in their seventies wore dusty suits and bolo ties and polished cowboy boots and weathered Stetsons. The old man's best friend, a plump elderly sheepherder recovering from a terrible bout with kidney stones, worked up a furious sweat moving the dirt atop his longtime companion. In past years the writer had often driven his aged amigo over to this man's camp west of the gorge during the hijadero. After the lambs were born, and the castrations had taken place, the trasquiladors came down from Colorado and sheared the entire flock in three days. As they shoveled on the dirt, he recalled how the old man had spent much of his youth in the early part of this century tending sheep on the surrounding mesas. During his teen years he had been a trasquilador, beginning on the ranches in southern Arizona in January, and moving north with spring, finally arriving to shear Montana sheep in June. He had loved the borregas, and was deeply attached to his few friends who still ran flocks in the valley. Of course, the herders were dying out. In ten more years they would all be gone.

After the grave was filled in, the men wandered away, returned to their pickups, drove off on the hard-packed snow. One of the old man's grandchildren, down from Denver, tried to arrange a funeral wreath just so on the mound of earth and stones. And juncos disported in the whitened piñon branches nearby, kicking down sprinkles and dusty puffs of snow.

Thirteen

When the weather cleared they went fishing. She was in a chipper mood, forging ahead on the path, sashaying back to him, giving little shoulder punches, sticking her tongue in his ear, whispering naughty propositions. It was about two miles from the rim of the gorge down to the river. Large pinecones littered the trail; juniper trees were heavy with blue berries. They stopped at his favorite giant ponderosa and got a whiff of the bark. It smelled strong, like vanilla.

The air was warm and languid after the rains.

She rubbed against him. He fondled her in all the appropriate places. She laughed and danced away. "Let's build it up to a fever pitch, then go crazy."

She galloped ahead, flicking her fingers at feathery Apache plume and bright yellow chamisa blossoms. Lizards, ignited by her shadow, scampered out of the way. Iridescent purple darning needles drifted to and fro.

He called her off the trail, and together they climbed about twenty feet up onto a ledge used by raptors for an eyrie. He explained, "Every spring for the last ten years great horned owls have nested here."

The rock was littered with tiny bones, owl shit, castings, little skulls, pack-rat droppings. In a crevice they found an egg that had never hatched back in April. Puffy fledge feathers were caught on jagged rocks and in the branches of yellow flowering brickellbush. Above their heads on the sheer rock wall were several hundred mud nests made by cliff swallows, now empty, of course, and silent.

They rested a moment, overlooking the gorge. "You have all these magic places," she said, growing moody and contemplative, opaque. "I envy you."

He pointed: "There's a buzzard." Then he told her that the birds singing in piñon trees below were Townsend's solitaires.

She hooked her hand through his arm and laid

her head against his shoulder. "Do you love me?" she asked.

"Yes . . . I love you," he answered.

She squeezed him a little, gently.

Down by the water, poison ivy had turned a bright crimson. Wild milkweed leaves were brilliant yellow. In places, Virginia creeper, flamboyantly red, was smothering the branches of ancient cedars. Watercress half filled the pool of an arsenic spring that emptied into the noisy river.

On a small beach where he liked to set up the rods, at least a dozen ebony-black tarantula hawks with bright orange wings were crawling around in a clump of sawgrass. Several of the wasps, caught in a mysterious torpor, lay at the base of the stems or on the sand, dying.

The more energetic wasps poked and prodded their logy comrades. They nudged and dragged and seemed almost to be performing artificial respiration. They were indifferent to the nearby humans.

"What's the matter?" she asked.

"I don't know. Some kind of poison? Perhaps it's a normal ritual of dying at the end of a season."

"Death again: Christ almighty!"

"They're beautiful."

"To a ghoul. C'mon, let's jam."

71

She grabbed one hand and yanked him upright. He groaned, "Oh my aching knees."

She whacked his arm. "Stop bitching," she said, and laughed. "I hate it when you complain."

"I'm *old*," he protested.

"In your brain, numskull. I think your body is wonderful!"

For almost twenty years he had fished the river, and he knew it well. He only used a few simple flies, tied by a friend, and moved quickly among the boulders heading upstream. Casting only to trout in back eddies or to holding spots behind rocks in midstream, he passed up most of the water, which was either too deep or too fast for his style. He used a tail fly and one dropper, fished almost on the surface, sometimes with a natural drift, or else skittered across the water. He danced easily across the massive basalt boulders, which were often more than ten feet high and shiny slick from the pummelings of roiling springtime runoff. She was more uncertain of her balance, and fell behind. "Hey," she cried, "you're supposed to be sick and dizzy! Wait up!"

But on the river he was in a familiar element, and the rhythm and momentum were important to his joy. Shadows needed to be on the water for fish to strike, which meant he had only two

hours before dark. So he concentrated wholly
on the task at hand, reading water, casting
quickly several times, then shifting his angle or
moving to another pool, hopping effortlessly
across the boulders.

"What happens if you fall?" she asked, catching
up, breathless and a trifle shaken.

"I never think of that," he said. "I'm not
afraid of anything down here."

The water was tinged a faintly green hue. It
moved fast, splashing against numerous boulders,
roaring loudly so they had to shout to hear
each other. But once into it he became all concentration
and quit talking. He always checked
out pockets on the near shore first, flicking his
small badger flies across the back eddies and any
quiet and shallow water behind a rock, or into
crevices where foam had gathered. Then he
climbed onto the higher outposts of stone and
cast across-stream with a precision she found
remarkable. He could land a fly exactly at the
base of rocks on the opposite shore, and more
often than not a fish struck instantly as the current
grabbed his line. He missed the first two
hits, but hooked a brown trout on the third. It
went into the air once and then swooped downriver
in fast, splashing water. He doubled back
downstream past the girl and worked the fish
quickly into a quieter pool, then guided it to his

net. She came over as he removed the hook, then held the foot-long trout beneath the surface, moving it forward and back, running water through the gills. When he let go, the fish slipped sideways, caught by the current, and was sucked into turbulent darkness.

She said, "You're good at this, aren't you?"

"If the conditions are right for my style, yes, I'm good at it. If conditions are bad, I'm a total flop. I hate to add weight for nymphing."

In the next forty-five minutes he landed and released over a dozen fish; the largest was about fifteen inches. She left him alone to enjoy his evening. His rhythm was fast and precise and fanatical. In almost the same motion that he released a fish he would straighten up and be casting again. He almost never stopped advancing. Every cast was directly aimed at a specific quarry, and almost always the cast triggered a strike. He failed to set the hook at least half the time, not from being slow, but because he was overeager—too fast. He laughed each time he failed, and moved on to the next position.

She had a hard time scrambling over enormous boulders, keeping up. The river banged, hissed, and splashed. Often as not he was silhouetted against angry spindrift, arm pumping, working that skinny line into a perfect cast. He felt absolutely comfortable, happy, on top of the world. And he had no idea if the girl was still behind him.

* * *

Shortly before dark the river went dead. He cast for another five minutes, just to be certain, then leaned against an enormous basalt slab and sighed deeply. "Shoot," he muttered, grinning contentedly, "it's all over." Almost languorously, he rubbed his eyes as if waking from an erotic dream.

Bats darted in silhouette against the narrow band of rosy sky. A canyon wren's haunting whistle descended the eastern cliff face, melodic and sorrowful. Fireflies floated on the dusky air, blinking as they headed nowhere. The wet roar of the river never ceased for a second, only now the water gleamed bright and silvery from the twilight atmosphere.

With darkness, sage bushes became hulking shapes. He took down his rod and slipped the reel into his knapsack. They reached a path above the river and started hiking out of the gorge on a carpet of pine needles. At the arsenic spring they drank fresh water and shared a Hershey bar. She kissed him lightly and said, "Thank you."

It was a long way to the top, and he climbed slowly. She reined in her energy and stayed beside him. A bright half-moon blotted out most of the individual stars except for those in the Big Dipper. And they could faintly discern a gauze of twinkles running north and south above the gorge—the Milky Way. In the west a bank of popcorn-shaped clouds had an eerie fluorescent sheen.

Now that the adrenaline had subsided, he was exhausted; they halted often. Several times she asked, "Are you okay?"

"Fit as a fiddle."

But even taking small steps and resting at regular intervals, he had trouble. The heart was bouncing around. His fatigued legs trembled; his calves came near to cramping. Sweat trickled under his collar, and salt stung his tongue when he licked his lips. At each descanso he leaned on his rod case and either gazed down at the river or up at the sky. It embarrassed him to be this weak. On the boulders he always forgot himself and was young again. Since childhood, he had loved to push beyond his own endurance.

She said, "Let's sit down here and take a long breather."

"No, no, I can make it fine. We're almost there."

At the top, they sat on the Dodge tailgate eating cucumber, Swiss cheese, and turkey sandwiches on dark German rye bread. They washed down the food with ice-cold beer. His hands were frozen, probably because of the blood-thinner pills, but he said nothing. His legs ached, but the food and beer tasted so good he would have sat there as long as the flavor lasted.

She said, "Do you think you could live with a person like me? Could you move to a college town? Would you follow me if I went to grad school at Chapel Hill or at Iowa?"

He knew how, but did not know how, to answer this question.

And so he waffled.

On the way south, heater whirring, she cuddled up against him. The warmth made his fatigue heavenly. KLSK played "The Unchained Melody," the Al Hibbler version. Singing along, he thought for a moment it could be 1958 and he was driving home at three in the morning with his steady girlfriend. She wore a cashmere sweater, a blouse with a Peter Pan collar, a circle pin, and a charm bracelet that he'd given her at Christmas. His trousers were stained from jism released during one of their marathon petting sessions.

To the depths of his weary bones, thirty-two years later, he remembered that special feeling.

Fourteen

That night they made love like this:

He entered her and then hardly moved. They were kissing almost without touching lips. Her fingers puttered against his shoulders as if reading braille, as if a faint electricity only she could decipher was wriggling off his skin. He pressed his mouth against her neck just below an ear and licked, tasting a fragrance not quite there. They were careful to be unsudden and thoughtful. When they shifted, the sheet rippled, cool and passive, stroking with clean white folds. After a while his tongue traced narrow paths across her body, in no hurry, avoiding all the obvious places. Still, wherever he went hurt like blessed needles. Her fingers rested in his hair, not guiding, merely touching because. She felt frail as a mouse pressed down upon by weight-less boulders, blissfully violated by an instru-ment of loving torture. The time to gloat was later. Quietly, he wrapped her hair around his fists, taking his own sweet time. Then slowly he bent her head backwards, almost underneath her body, straining to snap the neck. She arched her torso to the breaking point without a mur-mur or complaint, offering no resistance. In her heart, and in her cunt, a singing reached cre-scendo—

"God, I love you," she gasped.

"I love you too," she thought she heard him answer.

Fifteen

They shared another afternoon in the wilds. The climb began at twelve on a clear, humid day. Trees, rotting leaves, and knee-high grasses were damp from another shower. The world smelled earthen, slightly muggy. Flies and other small insects seemed passive, afloat in lethargy. At first, he had trouble with the heart: flip-flop rhythms, fibrillations, slight puffs of dizziness, traces of nausea. But then it warmed up and settled down. She kept well ahead, muted, plodding in and out of aspens, not near as restless as usual. Having taken a vow of silence (apparently), she rarely spoke. He remained quiet also, grateful for the serenity.

Each old lumber road intersection had a small spring. The first pool was circled by wild strawberries, white clover, and many small puffballs. Wild iris had gone to seed, and he fingered their twin pods, shaking loose minuscule black seeds. When she squeezed a puffball, velvet brown powder fine as smoke drifted casually off on the listless air.

Water left the second spring by an old wooden flume. With his toe he nudged coyote scat. Thimbleberry leaves were an iridescent ocher color, splotched with vivid red stains.

Three different paths diverged from the third spring. He stopped to pee. She never took a leak in the woods, and certainly not in front of him. Her melancholy was disturbing. Three fearless mountain chickadees puttered on a branch in front of his nose: black caps, black eye patches, black bibs. Their wings made fluttery noises.

A tall dead pine stood sentinel at the fourth seep. When three Clark's nutcrackers launched themselves from the highest branches, their wings made a mournful drumming sound, a kind of loud hollow chuffing. She followed them out of sight, unaware that he was staring at her.

* * *

They climbed away from the trickle of fresh water. Warm rich odors—of pine needles, grass, moist earth, elk droppings—arose from the road. They meandered through a single-file row of aspens. When five grouse jumped it happened so fast he never raised his weapon. She gave him a puzzled glance, but refrained from comment.

He left the road, traversing down a steep hillside, searching treetops for his birds. If the camouflaged grouse stayed quiet they were impossible to locate. Moss dangled off the lower dead evergreen limbs. Underfoot, premature spruce cones oozed gobs of glistening pitch. A grouse flapped, but in the dense foliage he never saw it. The ascent back up to the road almost killed him.

He rested, letting the sweat cool. She kneeled close by, poking at a cluster of bluebells. Her knees were scratched and bruised. He loved the thick white socks rolled down to the tops of her spotless aerobic sneakers.

"Are you okay?" he asked.

"Oh, leave me alone. Stop treating me like a baby. I can't stand your 'fatherly' tones."

"Hey, I am not—"

But then he let it slide, unwilling to promote a confrontation.

They circled higher. In spots the ground was soggy, rich in grass, crisscrossed by humps of gopher dirt. Other sections of old road were carpeted by green moss. At the seventh spring a jumble of downed trees was engulfed by spongy green matter interlaced with tiny white mushrooms. When she sipped the clear water, he warned, "It looks clean, but you could get giardia."

She shut him up with a beautiful glare. While she drank, he wandered off, checking the clover for grouse sign, happy to see Indian paintbrush in full bloom and yellow aspen leaves freckling the path. Fresh elk tracks proceeded in either direction. When a flicker retreated, his gun was up with the safety off before he realized it was not a game bird.

Drops of fresh water clung to her lips as she cupped one hand and lifted the hair away from her damp neck. He would have liked to kiss her youthful throat, but it was clear he must obey the distance between them.

Timothy reached up to their waists; oshá grew everywhere. At an overlook they stood among wheatgrass and blossoms of scarlet gilia, contemplating vast hillsides of flaming aspens across the canyons. Higher peaks in the distance were white from early snow.

On the road half a mile below them, three deer tiptoed along in stately grace, rumps high, big ears alertly cocked, as pristine as wild things ever get.

* * *

An hour later, lower than where the flock had first jumped, they flushed the birds again. He hit one about four feet off the ground going away; it banged off a thick aspen trunk and flapped in the grass for a few seconds.

"Nice shot, Adolf."

He sat on a log allowing his heart to calm down and paid her no mind. Brilliant purple asters lined either side of the route. They were about two hundred yards above the fourth spring. A water snake wriggled onto the road.

"Aren't you gonna kill it too?" she asked.

He had the grace not to answer.

They descended to an outcropping nearer the spring; aspen leaves floated on the water. The forest was quiet. In the blue sky lumpy white clouds remained stationary. He pushed her gently to the grass and without a word they made love. She climaxed in silence, dreamy and remote, and then uncharacteristically she held him very tightly for a moment. They heard feathers rustling and a few leaves ticking as they fell.

He could feel himself almost desperately begin to flood into her, but he cut it off quickly in self-defense. And he could feel her doing almost exactly the same thing in return.

Halfway down the mountain they stopped, puzzled by an angrily chattering red squirrel on a branch beside the road. Its complaint was aimed toward a spot deeper into the forest.

"Oh look—" She caught her breath.

A large hunchbacked bird hopped onto a dead log, giving an awkward flap of its wings to maintain balance. The big head stared at them, flared like a cobra and just as intense. The red squirrel scolded at a shrill pitch, but the bird seemed oblivious. Both humans confronted its eyes, and the hawk returned their attention, unblinking. A goshawk, he realized: only the third one he'd ever seen.

When it shifted higher onto the log they spotted a clump of red in the talons. Three minutes passed in a standstill, until the raptor lifted its wings, flapped once, and was airborne, headed directly at them. It flew out of the trees and crossed the road about ten feet away, clutching a dead squirrel whose tail whisked against grasses in passing. In absolute silence, the hawk reentered the forest of closely bunched aspen saplings and alders near the creek. It threaded effortlessly between all those impediments despite a wingspan that must have been four feet. Gliding as if inessential—a ghost—it disappeared into thicker timber . . . gone.

Sixteen

In a dream that night he lay beside her inside
a malleable, opaque sack or bubble. Call it
more of a placenta. The skin was thin and pat-
terned with delicate blue veins. They were
floating in nothingness. Through the sack
wall he could see blurred pinpricks of light,
which he surmised were stars. The thin mem-
brane rippled dangerously every time they
budged. It was about the size of a pup tent.
And constantly changed shape as they shifted
positions while undulating through the cold
universe. Though a peaceful mood prevailed,

he knew the sack was fragile and must not be punctured. Hence, they were in a dangerous predicament.

He wanted to screw her. She wore a baby-blue cashmere sweater and a 1950s high school skirt. Her legs were sheathed in nylons. Delicately, he touched her breasts. And went numb from the softness of her bosom translated through the giving fleece of cashmere. Cautiously changing position, he gingerly pushed up her skirt and fingered the slippery material of her panties. She groaned and pressed against him. He warned her to make no sudden gestures. Fear constricted all his movements.

Gradually, her panties grew damp against his fingertips. He poked the cloth back inside her vagina. She wanted to writhe, move, respond, but he forbade it. "Be careful, be careful." Rupture the bubble and they'd be sucked into the crushing vacuum of outer space.

She begged him to settle between her legs, but he dared not place them in more jeopardy. She had dark sorrowful eyes and a haunting ferret quality that kept him excited and hard. She had thin arms, narrow hips, skinny legs. He was terrified, and soon she became contemptuous of his restraint. They would never consummate their alliance.

He woke up, frustrated, yearning to complete the dream.

Beside him, the girl was sleeping quietly for a change. He slipped out of bed, padded into the bathroom and kneeled beside the tub, and there he released himself from bondage.

Seventeen

It was raining cats and dogs. They met for lunch at an organic joint and shared an avocado salad, with cups of cappuccino. She had on a red beret and a heavy black leather jacket, a pair of khaki shorts, and those same aerobic sneakers. "Come on," she said. "I'll walk you home, but then *I* have to get back to work. I'm hot, I'm on a roll at the typewriter, and I don't want to waste a minute."

But they'd hardly taken five steps when the rain doubled its intensity, and they ducked into the nearest doorway, which belonged to the only adult bookstore in town.

"My gosh," he joked, "look at all that paraphernalia. I don't believe it."

She tugged him by the hand. "Let's go in and have a look around."

"Are you kidding? You hate this kind of thing."

"There you go again." Petulantly, she yanked open the door. "Putting words in my mouth. Stop trying to control every little move I make, 'Dad.' "

They browsed the magazine racks. Together, they riffled through magazines with photo essays depicting any deviation imaginable. "I don't believe they get away with this stuff," he said. "When I was your age, my God, the girlie magazines were so tame."

" 'Girlie' magazines? What an old-fashioned word. When were you born, in the Pleistocene age?"

In back were some cubicles with pay video machines that showed pornographic movies. A quarter bought about a minute of visual sex. She wanted to have a look-see and led him by the hand. He changed ten dollars into quarters and they entered a booth. It was a pretty tight fit, about the size of two telephone booths, max. When he inserted a quarter, two well-hung and muscular young studs began to paw over a large-breasted woman, crudely ripping off her clothes, fondling her breasts, then biting them, then inserting their fingers—together—roughly in her ass.

She turned against him with a moan. "Oh Christ I love you—"

Astonished, he responded by kissing her viciously, shoving his hand down into her shorts and curling three fingers into her cunt while she fumbled to unzip his pants.

The film halted, so he fed in another quarter. A minute later he reached past her shoulder and inserted a fresh coin. By then she was standing naked, legs spread wide, leaning forward, bracing her hands on either side of the video screen while he screwed her from behind.

"Don't stop," she commanded. "This one is gonna be totally awesome."

"What is this all about?" he asked.

"Risk."

"I think it might be evil."

"Evil is exciting, you'll have to admit."

She was on top. She poked her sharp fingernail into the exact center of his left nipple and pressed down until it hurt, but of course he did not flinch. Then she placed her finger parallel between his teeth and said, "Bite me."

He bit down along the length of her finger, but not very hard.

"Harder."

He increased the pressure a little.

She said, "Mephistopheles was the most intelligent angel. That's why he was banished. Ask any brilliant person over the centuries, they all would rather have lived in hell. Heaven is boring. The moral universe is a dull universe. Who wants to be good? Harder."

"I said I don't want to hurt you."

"And *I* said harder."

He obliged. She put her left hand around his throat and squeezed, not too tightly, but enough to cause some discomfort. His right hand grasped her wrist, but made no effort yet to remove the hand at his throat.

"I'm going to have an exciting life. I like everything full-tilt. I don't care if I burn out early. You and me are two of a kind. Harder."

"No."

"Obey me, you fuck."

As his teeth clamped down more tightly, her right-hand fingers dug into his throat, almost making him choke. He grasped her wrist more securely. Her eyes glittered.

"I saw this Japanese film once called *In the Realm of the Senses*."

"I saw it too."

"What did you think of it?"

He said, "I liked it."

"Why?"

"I guess I felt that in a way I understood."

"I envied them. I envied the dude when she strangled him. I envied her when she was sawing off his cock. I envied their obsession and their passion and their willingness to follow it right straight down into hell."

"Yes."

"You're not hurting me enough, you wimp."

Her fingers tightened. He gagged a little and said, "If I break the skin you'll get an infection. Also, I could fracture the bone."

"I hope so. Something to remember you by. Our time is flying."

"No." His voice rasped out against the pressure of her thumb in his windpipe. Tears squeezed from her eyes.

She said, "You're a coward, a wuss, I despise you. Everything you do is play-acting, nothing is real, you only have courage in your books. You pretend to be bad but you're just a little boy in short pants. Your passion isn't real, it's make-believe. You're hopelessly old-fashioned. You always play it safe. You ditch women before the going gets tough. You're afraid to be evil. You're like a devil in Triple A ball, you'll never make the majors."

He yanked her hand from his throat and spit out her finger. She held the crippled hand against her chest, whimpering, grinning maliciously through her tears.

He said, "That was stupid. It had nothing to do with love."

"Wanna bet?"

* * *

"Just think, by the time I'm your age now, you'll be dead and gone, rotting in the grave."

"There's a thought." He grimaced. "Now lie back low and tuck your chin to your shoulder . . . yeah, that's good. Press your arms together against your tits, make 'em bulge up. Perfect. Wait . . . raise your right knee, higher—no, too high, drop it a little . . . there. Now hold it—"

Click.

"I'll come and leave things at your stone," she said. "Flowers, maybe. A grouse feather. Some shotgun shells. Talismans of your lust for blood. What else would you like?"

He advanced the film to the next frame. "How about some kisses? Put on lots of lipstick so that the print remains on my stone."

"I'll take off my panties, lipstick my vagina, and sit on your stone, leaving behind the impression of my cunt. I'll masturbate until the dates of your birth and death are slick with my secretions."

"Okay, now spread your legs, that's right. Scrooch sideways a little so your head's drooping over the edge. Keep the breasts together. I'll duck down here—that way your crotch, modestly covered by your fingers, will be blurry in the foreground. We'll be looking up your torso toward those delectable little mams—"

"Maybe I'll just piss on your grave. Or shit on it in anger. This is incredible, what you're doing. What a pig."

Click.

"I'm told they defecate daily on the grave of Kazantzakis on Crete."

He tugged her by the ankle back onto the bed and inserted himself.

She said, "Just think. You'll be stuck underground, riddled with worms, while I'm hot in the throes of passion, fucking some young stud. Cold icy snow will cover your grave while sweat makes my breasts and belly slimy."

"Keep squeezing them." He focused and depressed the shutter release button a few more times. "I like it. You look like a real teeny-bopper slut today."

"You make me feel like a slut. You're horrible."

"Good."

Click.

Eighteen

In bed, even while asleep, she was terribly restless. She tossed and twisted and yanked the sheet
and all the blankets over to her side. She lay on
her stomach, spread-eagled, then suddenly
curled into a fetal position, which she held for
a few minutes only. Then she was on her back,
knees up, knees down—she flung out her arms
and an elbow, crashing against his chest, waking him up. If he dared to snore, she banged his
arm until he woke. Sometimes she pinched his
nose and he became conscious with a jolt, suf-
focating, ridiculed by her laughter. "Christ, you

make a lot of noise," she groused. "It sounds like you're dying. I hate it."

"I'm not used to sleeping with another person."

She conked out instantly, holding him, an arm across his chest, her leg, pinning down his thigh, bent into his crotch. He could not go to sleep while touching . . . while touching anybody. He lay quietly, feeling her against him. Pretty soon she stirred, groaned, smacked her lips, and began to squirm. She was asleep and her restless shenanigans began again.

Nineteen

On the mesa, thanks to frequent rain, water filled many stock ponds. They went out there to hunt migratory birds with his camera. The absolute lack of trees provided a dramatic change of pace. After the complexity of forest terrain, the simplicity of a sagebrush plain was almost intimidating. In the sky, massive cloud formations seemed born of silent and harmless atomic explosions: they boiled joyfully in dramatic slow motion. Heat lightning quivered behind the eastern mountains.

They settled in the lee of an embankment, below the wind, beside a puddle thirty yards across. Tire tracks leading to the water had been made by tank trucks loading up for thirsty sheep.

She hunkered down against the barren plain, uncomfortable in such an exposed position. Three nighthawks glided back and forth, snagging just-born bugs. During lulls in the wind, they could see insects departing their larval sheaths, leaving circular ripples on the water when they escaped toward heaven. Several bats also chased the furiously hatching meals. At times, so many ripples dotted the surface it seemed as if rain was falling.

Neither of them spoke. As the sky darkened, the wind abated completely. Nighthawks and bats zigzagged in bursts of frenetic motion, all of it totally mute. A pair of doves landed on the far side and ambled along the waterline, sipping a little, in no hurry. Then a killdeer appeared and set to work busily stabbing for morsels in the mud.

Puffy clouds whirled and danced in a torpor of cumulus mayhem, and light splintered in all directions, seamless and defiant as the sun lowered from sight. For a moment sagebrush was laminated in a rich golden color, then only the mountains east of town reflected crepuscular glory.

Six phalaropes arrived without splashing and began swimming aggressively, working as a team, plucking stuff from the water. None of the other diners paid any attention.

"How can so much activity be so quiet?" she whispered. "The noisiest thing out here is mosquitoes being born."

After an inaudible *ping!* a circle formed on the water, then a nighthawk swerved and dipped: bye-bye bug. The insects had a life expectancy of about one second.

"Nature," she griped cheerfully, quoting Woody Allen. "It's just a great big restaurant."

In earnest whispers she asked him more questions about writing. Already she had expressed a desire to learn everything he cared to share about inventing books. "I want to be a great writer one day." They'd had numerous discussions about momentum, language, plot and structure, style and rhythm. He rarely supplied her with satisfactory answers. Many times he had reiterated, "With me it's always been a process of hit or miss. I can never figure things out ahead of time. I have instincts, but I'm not very articulate about them. I just leap right in and bull ahead willy-nilly. All my life I've had almost no discipline, but a boundless energy. I create thousands of pages, then try to twist them into shape through countless rewrites. Sometimes, if I'm lucky, and I persevere, I stumble onto a novel that works. But not often. I've written about sixty books, maybe, but only published twelve. I wish I had a different system. This one, which I invented when I was pretty young and energetic, doesn't work so hot now because I'm kind of worn out. But I don't know how to change."

He denigrated his own work. "I always begin with such grandiose hopes; I always wind up just trying to salvage a novel."

She said, "I love jumping into things head-first, not knowing at all what will happen. I don't care if I burn out early. I just really want to live."

He admitted, "Me too. I used to love leaping before I looked. I guess that's why I got remarried after living alone for twelve years."

She squeezed his arm. "That's why we're here together, staring at this funny little puddle, isn't it?"

"Yes."

Although he thought he knew exactly what would happen. And isn't it sad when life boils down to such prescience—?

Darkness enveloped them. One minute the sky was blue and starless; seconds later it was black and freckled with bright diamonds. Coyotes howled over in another arroyo; their bloodcurdling yips set his heart on fire. Wild animals still exist apart from the human race. Thrilled, he smiled childlike to hear them. She squeezed his hand.

A chill settled on the plain. They embraced, feeling very close, pressing against warm silken dirt. The phalaropes, bats, and nighthawks continued feeding by starlight. Occasionally, a nighthawk sliced down low, almost ticking them with its sharp wingtips. Hesitantly, they kissed, almost shyly, and with consideration. It was one of those breath-held moments when neither dared up the ante. Their lips only brushed, without pressure or urgency, yet their bodies were soft and melting. Though they held their eyes open, neither could see the other. Crickets began to stir and click, but not insistently; an autumn shiver had soothed the mesa.

They hugged quietly. He smelled in her hair a faint residue of clean shampoo. She touched her lips against his neck, where an artery was pulsing, and said, "Thank you."

Twenty

He listened quietly as she recounted another installment of her future novel:

It seems that when the child, Maria, was only six years old, she had traveled to Spain and was chosen to be La Princesa de la Alcachofa, the Princess of the Artichoke. This ceremony took place in a small whitewashed town about an hour inland from the Mediterranean between Valencia and Alicante. You will remember that Maria had fluffy blond hair, bright blue eyes, knobby knees on skinny legs. They dressed her all in white lace with a silky ribbon in her hair.

Then she stepped inside a tin artichoke, and when they pulled some wires the petals folded up around her. Though it was dark and stifling hot inside, she was excited and unafraid. She clung tightly to the center pole. The artichoke was attached to a hoist-and-pulley rig in the small plaza. Everyone had gathered for this celebration, the town's annual fiesta. All the peasants wore berets, and red sashes around their waists, and white trousers, and rope-soled alpargatas. Slowly, they raised the artichoke high in the air. When it stopped, the petals opened. And when the people saw the little girl up there, they hushed. Then Maria began to sing.

She had a pure and heavenly voice, like an angel floating above them. The onlookers hardly dared twitch or brush away a fly. She sang the "Ave Maria" as if it were a personal message from the magic land of God to everyone here on earth. The people began to weep . . . and the sky was blue, too blue. . . .

"To the child, all her long and tantalizing life lay far ahead, forever."

She laughed in delight, but he avoided her eyes and turned his head away.

Twenty-one

It was raining again. She had invited him over
to her room at the foundation, and they had
built a cedar fire and snacked on graham crack-
ers and chamomile tea. He sat in a chair by the
window, gazing into the storm while she
touched the bow to her violin and played the
sweetest music he'd ever heard, a high forlorn
melody that broke his heart. It seemed very important not to watch as she played. He had no
wish to disturb her in any way that might break
the spell. So he remained stationary while raindrops splashed against the window and tree

leaves fluttered in the wind. Then he closed his eyes and pictured making love to his soon-to-be-ex-wife on that mattress placed between boxes of redolent apples. Sometimes he felt sad and guilty and pitied her; on other occasions the sorrow was for himself. He would never irrigate the two small fields again, or go to ditch meetings with people he had grown to love over the past twenty years. He would never watch grackles on the bird feeders out the kitchen window while he typed on a novel. He would never see hummingbirds at those hollyhocks—

He had finished typing the revised divorce papers. Now he should file the petition and make an appointment to see the judge. It would probably take only a minute. What a world where you sign a piece of paper and land disappears from your possession—poof! And your emotions toward another person are supposed to be entirely changed.

Suddenly, he began to cry. He had not shed a tear in ages. She quit playing the violin, and he heard the brushstrokes of her body rustling about the room. The fire crackled, wind howled, raindrops splashed against glass. He tasted, on his lips, honey from the tea. Then her fingertips landed almost without weight on his shoulders.

"What's the matter?"

"Nothing. Your music is beautiful."

He doubled over and really began to sob.

"Are you all right?" She kneeled close to him, but still he would not open his eyes.

He muttered inanely, "I just feel sad."
She kissed him and said, "Me too."

Later, she had a suggestion:

"I don't have to leave on the twenty-third. I could take the semester off. I really like it out here. I might find a little place like yours and get a job. I only need a minute to find work. I can con anybody into coughing up some bucks."

He clenched inside. "What about momentum? Isn't it hard to start up again in school once you've stopped for a while?"

She tossed her head impatiently. "Nobody goes straight through college these days. Everyone quits to work, travel, get married, have a nervous breakdown, enter a detox center."

He shifted uncomfortably. "It all seems so fragile now." His son had dropped out after one semester. His daughter had taken a year off between high school and college. "In my day we went right through—one, two, three, four. It was a helluva lot cheaper that way."

She said, "Don't worry, I'd lead my own life. I want to complete my novel. I wouldn't get in your hair."

"Oh no, that's not a problem. Only . . ."

"Only what?"

"Only . . . I worry about you," he said. "You're close to a degree. But it's very easy to get sidetracked. It seems real important for you to grab the education while you can."

After a slight pause, she agreed. "Yeah. That makes the most sense, doesn't it?"

Twenty-two

Toward the end of her stay, they drove up north to flatlands near the Colorado border.

While they walked along a sandy arroyo, nearby sprinklers in an alfalfa field came on with a loud grating sound, then a wet droning, almost a whine. The spray fizzed for about ten minutes, then stopped. In the silence they heard magpies chattering. A few hawks were soaring.

"It makes me sad, all this mechanical irrigating," he said.

She was back in snotty form: "Sorry, I forgot my violin."

"They suck it up from the aquifers until the water is depleted. They're doing it all over the earth. The soil is leached out, and salts gather, destroying the dirt. In 1900 we had an average of two feet of rich topsoil in America, up to six feet in places. Today the average is down to six inches."

"Thanks. I was really enjoying this day."

"I can't help it," he said. "It makes me angry, frustrated. Nobody really gives a damn."

"Except you. Dangling up there on your stupid cross."

"It isn't just me," he said uncomfortably, tired of being on the defensive.

"I know. Ralph Nader, Barry Commoner, Rachel Carson, Wendell Berry, Anne Ehrlich—your gods. Spare me, okay? I'm not supposed to be back in school until the twenty-seventh."

He shut up. It was useless to complain, and he hated all the confrontation. They walked through a sparse thicket of dry, leafless willow saplings that had been stripped by hungry cattle a month ago. A dove fluttered up from a sandbar, and he shot it. As he bent over to retrieve the bird, she said, "Bully for you."

He glanced at her. There was a sexual glint in her eye. He undid the burlap bag tucked into his knapsack shoulder strap and slipped in the dove.

They followed a line of old cottonwoods, she on the eastern edge in shadow, he on the west. Small birds darted among the willow thickets—

juncos, sparrows, some migrating warblers. They flushed a Cooper's hawk, nothing else. The hawk circled and landed in the same place behind them, unafraid.

In fact, the raptors had no fear whatsoever.

The cottonwoods met a stand of willows in a V at the point of a triangle. Within the triangle were several acres of chest-high flowering rabbit brush. They turned, heading southwest toward the sun. The sky was magnificent. A complete rainbow arced over the nearby mountains. Enormous gray-and-white clouds were bursting in vibrant explosions of vapor behind the sierra. Between clouds the sky was periwinkle blue.

He'd never seen a rainbow like this one, which even held its colors against patches of blue. Not a single break flawed the arc, even where no moisture was visible. Lightning flickered over the mountains. The bright wet-sulfur yellow of rabbit brush flowers was gaudy and sensational in the sunset light. High above, against the rainbow, several dozen nighthawks were cruising. Closer by, first a redtail, then a Cooper's, then a sharp-shinned hawk passed overhead, eyeing them lazily, unafraid.

He said, "Jesus, this is gorgeous."

"I think 'gaudy' is a more appropriate adjective."

Eagerly, he said, "Let's go over to that grass and make love."

She snorted sarcastically. "Surely you jest."

He opened his side-by-side, removed the shells, set down the gun, and raised both hands in a gesture that encompassed the universe.

"You *never* saw a sky like this!"

"In every cornball *National Geographic* special I see a sky like this."

He laughed, not to be deterred. "I'm gonna come in my pants it's so special."

"Ejaculation *praecox*."

That touched a nerve. "I feel sorry for your generation," he said, not unkindly. "I grew up in an age where it was a thrill to be awed."

"There you go again: Mr. Superior."

"But doesn't this"—and he waved his hand at everything—"touch you in any way at all?"

"Like a Walt Disney movie, sure. Or the poems of Rod McKuen. We ought to play a little Barry Manilow in the background."

Putting an arm around her shoulders, he bent his head and nuzzled at the nape of her neck. She smelled fuzzy, of dust and of sunshine. Also slightly medicinal—sage. He licked, tasting salt. She squirmed. "That tickles."

On the other side of the cottonwoods a hawk shrieked. Sparrows in nearby branches froze for about five seconds, then recommenced their twittering.

When the rainbow slowly evaporated, dark clouds massed together and lightning flashed more emphatically. Out in the open he was terrified of electrical storms, and here they were totally exposed.

"Let's take a powder." He shuffled forward at a quicker pace. The truck was parked near an arroyo about half a mile away.

"What's the hurry?" she called gaily, deliberately lagging behind.

"The hurry is I don't want to be fried alive."

"I *love* lightning." She reached up to touch it with eager fingers.

"Hey . . . come on. Don't be stupid."

He knew that from the rear his gait must look farcical, but it was as fast as he could travel. He could not push the heart any harder without it being dangerous. Hunched over to make himself less of a target, he heard her peals of laughter.

"You look like a lobster!" she called.

I look like a whimpering old fool, he corrected, ashamed. But when another lightning streak crackled, followed by a crushing detonation of thunder directly overhead, he gave a little hop, almost squealed, and dropped down fast in order to scramble under the lowest strand of a barbwire fence.

"Move it or lose it," he cried, humiliated by the growing distance between them. He knew it was okay to be afraid, but that didn't help. The truck was still a good hundred yards distant. The lollygagger was strolling with her head held high, a perfect target. As he glanced back, jagged streaks of electricity danced behind her and his neck hair frizzed in terror. The explosions seemed to ignite her, but she never twitched. He could love her so much it broke his heart. No, not love, he corrected, scrambling as fast as he dared toward safety . . . excitement. That's all it was, excitement.

"*Now* I want to fuck!" she yelled. "Right here, right now. If you refuse, we'll never screw again."

Why bother to answer?

Yes, if he had any guts they would make love right now in the sandy arroyo, daring the elements to kill them. But he wasn't that crazy anymore.

He wanted to live longer than seemed in the cards, given his various ailments.

By the time he reached the truck, the landscape was black, brooding, ominous. A few raindrops spattered. He shed the pack, dropped his gun behind the seat, then grabbed it again and removed the shells. He placed the gunnysack with eight doves in it into the bed and hopped behind the wheel—safe!

She came along walking deliberately, apparently out for a stroll, obnoxiously unafraid. More lightning cavorted jaggedly behind her. *Oh Jesus*, he prayed, *don't let her die*. Another part of him wished for her fiery doom. He wondered: How long can she keep it up before they break her spirit? How long before she grew tired of his fatigue and told him "Sayonara"?

He remembered being twenty and dancing through blizzards wearing only a T-shirt.

At the truck, while she took her own sweet time climbing inside the cab, he couldn't help himself: "Thank God you made it. I hate lightning. It terrifies me."

"So I noticed."

"On the other hand," he said, hoping to sound jocular, "only a pretty dumb cunt would expose herself like you just did."

He expected her to lash back. But, as always, she outfoxed him, impossible to predict. "Actually, I was terrified," she admitted. "I just wanted to see if I could do it. I wanted to make you feel small. But look, I peed in my pants."

Twenty-three

He twisted the cap off a beer. Yes, he was taking verapamil and Quinaglute and Coumadin to control the heart arrhythmia and keep his blood thin, and the doctors had forbidden alcohol. But he loved to drink, especially an ice-cold beer after the hunt, and so had decided to hell with it a long time ago. Sometimes, reacting to the Quinaglute, alcohol gave him a terrible headache. But for a while beforehand the treat would be exquisite.

She put ice, vodka, and Diet Coke into a Styrofoam coffee cup. They clinked "glasses."

"To September."

She grinned broadly: "To your corny rainbow."

They drank. He was almost too grateful for being alive on this wonderful afternoon.

A gusting wind rocked the truck in its blustery gales. Rain—quickening into a noisy deluge—clattered against the tin roof. It all happened so quickly and contained the violence of a nasty blow. Lightning lit up everything, slashing to earth in many places at once. The truck shivered. Thunder ruptured heaven directly overhead, then all hell broke loose, hailstones slamming down.

"Christ almighty!" he yelled, but he couldn't even hear himself. Lightning flared almost continuously on every side, white-hot and electric, flung earthward by the booming. Visibility ceased entirely except for those electric shocks quivering inside the massive pounding of hail. The noise was unbearable. He'd never experienced a similar violence, and his heart thundered, terrified. Hail battered the truck; he thought sure all the glass would shatter. Ice balls big as his thumb pummeled the front hood, bouncing crazily in all directions. What a tumultuous beating! He was sweating, fighting to keep his heart from freaking out. Joyfully she screamed at him, but he could hear nothing. She screamed again to no avail. All he could think to wonder was: Do rubber tires protect you in a car? He made sure not to touch the door or the steering wheel, which might conduct electricity. He was so afraid he wanted to burst out crying.

When she grabbed the cooler that sat between them and banged open her door to tumble it out, dozens of icy white bullets ricocheted inside, stinging his thighs. She hauled shut the door, then pulled off her T-shirt and wriggled out of her shorts and panties. Deliriously happy, yelling at him, who was deaf from the battering noise, she pointed at her crotch, then reached out, leaning back, and pulled him between her thighs.

"You're crazy!" he bellowed, still unable to hear himself.

Her lips moved as she screamed back inaudibly. The clattering of hail intensified. They seemed to be inside a roaring explosion that would never end. He thought the pounding would drive him crazy. The truck was shaking frantically, as if the next mighty gust would tumble it over. They were reflected against each other in brilliantly sizzling light.

She was so wet he almost fell inside. God, he was scared! She screamed at full decibels, unhearable, and the thunderstricken world rocked dangerously as they fucked.

His ears couldn't stand it any longer; for sure the cab was going to capsize. He closed his eyes, but through the veined membranes could see her face lit up by fiery dazzlements. Utterly terrified, he came in huge, spastic contractions, as if he were twenty-two again with all the joy in the world to squander.

It stopped on a dime. The wind quit, the clatter abated, the lightning receded. Thunder rumbled from a distance, saying good-bye. As if in mockery, streaks of sunshine lighted up a different planet: all around them lay the white of winter—at least two inches of hail. And a silence that seemed devoid of noise. The temperature had dropped remarkably.

He said, "I don't believe it."

Naked, she opened the door and got out, standing beside the truck for a moment, calculating the universe. Then she leaned inside, reaching behind the seat, and lifted out his gun case. She unzipped it, removed the L.C. Smith, and laid the case on the seat. She broke open the gun and inserted two shells, then stood a while longer beside the truck, scanning the country-side now so radically altered. Several doves flew quickly down the arroyo. The sky boasted a thousand dramatic cloud formations. In spots, sunshine glittered blindingly off white ice.

She meandered about thirty yards in front of the truck and hesitated. Her young body was firm, slightly chunky, powerful. *The world exists only for twenty-year-olds,* he thought. He realized that he would never forget this naked girl holding a gun in all that empty space, silhouetted against the emotional sky. He had a camera, but dared not risk a photograph.

She raised the gun and pointed skyward, sighting. He followed her line: a large hawk was circling. He was thinking, *Of course she won't pull the trigger,* when she fired. Feathers puffed around the raptor and it flapped its enormous wings heavily, holding in place until her second blast took its life. The wings went lax and the redtail fell like a rock, trailing feathers against the radiant sky. White beads of hail splashed in all directions when it smashed to earth.

His heart had dived with the hawk.

She sauntered over and took an arrogant stance above it, looking down. Then she broke open the gun and settled it in the crook of her arm as she stooped, lifting her prize. She faced him, spreading the wings, displaying the enormous sagging hawk in an irreverent posing attitude: *Look at my macho trophy.*

He was too stunned to react. She grinned and held the painful grin for a long time. A huge black rain cloud was forming behind her, nearer the mountains. It remained absolutely silent until he heard the cries of geese and soon spotted a large V of them flying low, moving across the horizon behind her. She never turned to acknowledge them. He was baffled by everything. Finally he heard her voice:

"Hey, look at me. I *got* it!"

As, slowly, mischievously, she walked back under his dazed eye, he could think only that he hated her. And had a question to ask: Why? She dumped the redtail in the pickup bed, then leaned into the cab to retrieve her clothes and dressed slowly, pausing often to regard the ever-changing weather conditions. Her skin was blue and goose-pimpled, but she refused to acknowledge the discomfort. She was enjoying his confusion. More stately geese flew by, and at least a half-dozen other medium to large hawks circled above the fields of stubble, seeking miniature prey.

After she had entered the truck, shut the door, and started mixing another vodka, he said quietly, "Get rid of it."

"No."

"You don't know how against the law it is to kill one of those. We'd be fined a million dollars."

"You're not telling me anything I don't know."

"It would be awful. Front-page news in all the papers."

"So what?"

"For starters, they'd crucify me."

"Do you ever think of anyone except yourself?"

"Why did you do it?" he finally managed to ask. "To ridicule me?"

"I like the risk."

"It's a protected species."

"Precisely. I wanted to see if you'd hate me."

"It worked. I hate you."

"Good. Now you know how I feel. I was getting tired of your Goody Two Shoes act. A hawk is no better or worse or deserving of life than a dove or a grouse or a trout."

It wasn't hatred, actually; it was more like a profound despair. He had a strong urge to cry. He also had an erection and wanted to make love again.

"You really can't take it home with us."

"Sez who?"

He was amazed at her audacity, and her audacity was always a turn-on. He stepped outside, retrieved the hawk, and carried it over to a cluster of willow saplings. The bird weighed less than he would have expected. All its bones were hollow, most of its bulk was feathers. Sick at heart, he tossed it unceremoniously into the thicket. A smaller hawk, circling overhead, screeched. A few teal flew by quickly, heading north toward the reservoir. He hoped never to kill anything again.

★ ★ ★

As they headed away on a dirt road she said, "Nothing really affects you, does it? You're dead inside. You're a complacent old fart. You're like a zombie. You're afraid to stand up for what you believe in. You're afraid to hit me. You're so fucking polite you make me puke."

Then she leaned over and opened his fly and began to suck him. Moments later he pulled over and they made love. It was rough and spectacular. He was lost and helpless in a place he'd always wanted to visit but had never had the guts to try. He raped her in hatred and she clawed him back.

Fear made the orgasms wonderful.

But as soon as it was over she began to cry. Tears poured out of her, and although she tugged on a sweatshirt and a down jacket, she couldn't keep from shivering, and her teeth chattered. When they returned to the road he put the heater on full blast, but it did no good. Finally, he glided onto the shoulder and braked.

"Are you okay?"

"Do I look okay?"

He reached for her, but she pushed his hand away.

"Leave me alone. I don't want to touch you, ever again."

He said, "I'm sorry."

"Yeah, I bet you are."

Twenty-four

On September 23 the genie returned to her bottle, and the bottle disappeared on a shuttlejack
headed south to the airport. All she left behind
was a short piece of writing faintly scented by
her perfume. At first he could not read it. Then
he *would* not read it. He thought of tearing it
up, but resisted that temptation. Forget his personal emotions, he still possessed a professional
curiosity. But he delayed the reading for a while,
trying to sort through what had happened. Yet
it was impossible to concentrate. He meandered,
unable to face it. Instead, he remembered that

on this day seventeen years ago Pablo Neruda had died. He got out Neruda's *Veinte Poemas de Amor* and began to browse through the poet's passionate love for women.

> *Body of a woman, white hills, white thighs, you look like a world, lying in surrender. . . .*

Quickly, he put down the book, ashamed at his own shortcomings.

After that he dawdled and sat still, lay down for a nap, but could not sleep. Finally, after dark, he opened the envelope and read her story.

"X loves a man older than her father. The problem is, he's dying. He used to be young and an athlete, but of course that's all over now. None of this matters to her, however. But with him it's a great weight he cannot slide off his shoulders. He is ashamed of his own weaknesses and intimidated by her youth. Even at this late date, he still thinks it's his obligation to be immortal. She could care less and would gladly have put school, career, even her sexuality on a back burner in order to be with him if only he had the guts to untether his passion, whatever the cost. But he fears the price will be his life and cannot muster. Almost from the start she sees in him this reticence, and realizes her heart will soon be broken. No matter, she decides to take a risk, then live with the pain forever. True love is rare enough in this day and age and for whatever odd reasons she feels true love for his crippled being. He fights her every step of the way, yet shares with her some of the beauty that moves him. Nevertheless, his fluttering heart is in a cage and she cannot reach it. To his credit he does not ask for pity, and she has none to give. In the end he is an empty promise, and she never opens the gift of herself for him to savor. All the same, when it's over she feels a terrible pain inside, a stab of fire and ice at the center of her being, which may never go away. Yes, X is still young and foolish, but in spite of that she has the wisdom to realize that only rarely in her life will her own heart be touched as vividly by another person. Too bad, however—the moment is over. They made a choice, life goes on, why be bitter?"

He read the piece over several times. It made him angry—she didn't understand . . . then it made him sad. "No," he said aloud. And then, "Yes." Then he didn't know what to think about it or how to shape a reply. He was ashamed. If only he could explain—

That night he lay in bed unable to sleep, writing her a long letter in his mind. He apologized, then retracted the apology. He defined all kinds of love. Well, she was just too young, that's all. Around three o'clock he finally took a pill and fell asleep.

Next day he wrote a long letter to the girl. He typed for almost an hour, speaking of small daily tribulations, an odd comment overheard at a café, a flock of geese that had passed high overhead while he was on his bike near the bank. He wanted to say other things but was oddly intimidated, off-balance, reluctant. Of course he asked about her health, he worried. It seemed tacky to end with great protestations of love, and so, although that was how he felt, he certainly never mentioned it. Then he typed her address on an envelope, inserted the letter and sealed it, and pedaled over to the post office.

After the letter was gone he wanted it back. Well, he could write her another. No, it was better just to let sleeping dogs lie.

In the distance, thunder rumbled. Confused, he wondered if it might snow.

Twenty-five

In the morning he woke up early and set off on his bike to finish the divorce. His wife had signed and notarized the property settlement agreement and the Waiver of Appearance. He had an appointment with the judge at ten-thirty. But the judge did not appear until almost eleven, and then he was in a hurry. He browsed through the papers and signatures in about five seconds, signed on the dotted line, and said, "Well, on to a new stage of life." They shook hands and he was out of there.

He went next door to have the quit-claim deed

notarized by a clerk of the county, made a Xerox, and put the original in an envelope for his wife. Ex-wife. Then he pedaled south to the motor vehicle department and got papers for transferring the title of the Impala over to his wife. Ex-wife. Next, he had a notary at the Xerox place in town sign and stamp papers transferring water rights on the land to his wife. Ex-wife. Finally, he went to the gallery where she would report to work later that afternoon and left the envelope on her desk with instructions on how to file the deed, the water rights, and the change of title. He explained she would have to stop by the insurance agency and switch the Impala onto a policy of her own, for which he'd included a check.

After that, it was done. He was a free man, and out one car, one-point-eight acres of land, and the house he loved and had lived in for twenty years. His personal property now consisted of a pickup truck with a hundred and twenty-two thousand miles on the odometer, four thousand dollars in the bank, and perhaps five thousand dusty, tattered paperback books in a storage locker that rented for fifty-five bucks a month.

He experienced neither relief nor anger. He felt numb.

How did a person cope with such loss? Maybe he should have kicked her out, fighting for everything that belonged to him. She had only lived there five years. She had never put in a cent of her own money. She *had* no money, she had nothing at all. She'd had him for a husband, but now he was gone and he felt sorry for her. Whether it was right or wrong, smart or stupid, the decision was made; he had chosen to give up his home. And he believed that you don't cry over spilt milk. You turn your back and move on.

He pedaled north for a couple of miles, almost choking to death on gas fumes from a steady stream of traffic. He was going nowhere, aimless and distracted. The wind and the pollution and the dust stung his eyes, that's why he started crying. At the blinking light he turned around and cruised back to his apartment, snagged an apple, and went inside to brush his teeth. He set his bridge on a ledge below the mirror and assessed his features. *I look old,* he thought. During the last few years his eyebrows had grown bushy, salt-and-pepper, kind of snarly. He was embarrassed. A tangle of ridiculously long white hairs sprouted helter-skelter out of his earlobes. On several occasions, antagonized, he had clipped them. But they grew back overnight, and so he decided to leave well enough alone.

He made a face at himself, then grinned stupidly minus the two front teeth. It was a silly image, and he giggled.

"What, *me* worry—?"

Twenty-six

It rained during the night, and when he awoke the day was overcast and grainy. The moisture had turned to snow sometime early in the morning. A wet layer of white lay across the green grass, and all the bright red apples on his small tree wore dunce caps of powder.

A chill was in his bones as soon as he got out of bed. His wrists ached from being bent over sharply as he slept, and the knuckles on his right hand were swollen and throbbing with arthritic pain. He needed another load of wood for winter, and decided in spite of the weather to go for it.

He dressed quickly and went to a café, where he had two cups of tea in front of a fire and read the Sunday newspaper. Then he was warm and drove south out of town. The sun shone brightly on the deserted road. Snow decorated yellow cottonwoods alongside the stream. Slivers of ice protruded onto the still water behind beaver dams. Clusters of orange willows were frosted by snow, and webs of the white stuff connected the culms of tall grasses in fields on either side of the river.

What a sparkling day! He clicked on the radio to a professional football game. With the taste of honey lingering in his mouth, he admired the fiery blaze of cottonwood foliage against evergreen hillsides now transformed by silver powder. Three ravens flew off the shoulder as his truck approached. A half mile later he passed another bunch of the enormous black birds shivering in a gully off the shoulder. They did not blink as he zoomed past.

When fans went crazy over an intercepted pass, he experienced a nostalgic thrill from his athletic boyhood.

He entered a narrow canyon and slowed to a crawl on the rugged dirt road. In places the lack of stones or gravel made traction difficult. His Dodge slithered. After barely a mile he decided it would be impossible to reach his regular wood area. So he backed cautiously down a wet incline and spun around in a steep turnout, riding the clutch and spinning his wheels in the sloppy terrain. But he managed to park more or less on the level and headed in the opposite direction, and decided to gather whatever wood he could scavenge in the area.

He was at the bottom of a clearing on a steep hillside. In the middle was a clump of scrub oaks, their leaves a golden-brown color. Tall ponderosas circled the clearing, their branches heavy with snow. Scattered stalks of woolly mullein, oddly furred, had an apple-green hue.

He listened to the game a while longer, touched by the announcer's familiar rhythms. At seven, he had first crouched by a radio during a World Series game between the Brooklyn Dodgers and the New York Yankees. Ever since, he had loved the electronic transmission of sports. Always, in a vehicle, he fiddled with the radio dial to locate a game, any sort of game. Baseball, football, hockey, basketball— it only mattered that a contest was going on, that the announcers had enthusiasm, that you could hear a crowd in the background. It could be a professional event, or college, high school, Little League. All that mattered was that it be a game.

* * *

Eventually, he clicked off the radio, donned scruffy leather gloves and a woolen cap, and went to work. The sun came and went, playing peekaboo. As he gathered wood, the snow was melting. Woodcutters had selectively harvested the area eight to ten years ago, but most of their leavings had been scavenged over, and many of the remaining bits and pieces were too rotten for burning. His gloves were soon soaked, and his hands grew icy. He stopped from time to time, shoving fingers into his crotch to warm them up. As he waited, water dripped off leaves and branches, a steady, comforting sound. From higher up came the fussbudget mewling of Clark's nutcrackers, or perhaps Steller's jays, he could never tell for sure.

He worked hard, always moving, stooping, picking up branches, chunks of wood, busting off flimsy twigs by smashing them against the solid trunks of nearby trees. He lofted the pieces downhill toward the truck. Because the wood was widely scattered, he had to climb thirty or forty yards above the truck, tossing his harvest down in relays. At one point he had climbed so high it required three relay stations to fling the wood to his truck. But he enjoyed tossing the missiles. He flipped all the smaller chunks underhand, in a high arc, end over end downhill.

He was so accurate the wood usually fell within a few feet of the truck. Larger branches he sailed off sidearm; they spun like rotor blades of a helicopter. The largest branches he propelled as if tossing a javelin, or the caber.

He soon discarded the gloves, preferring to feel wood against his flesh regardless of splinters or the cold. Hats, too, he had always disdained, and soon the woolen cap was gone.

Sometimes he found a "bomb," a small chunk of wood with yellow and green veins of sap, almost as heavy as a rock. He hefted its weight, looking forward to the moment it would roar into flames as soon as he touched a match. The old man used to ram over dead stumps with the front bumper of his pickup truck because the stumps were often rich in trementina. The old man had taught him a love of wood gathering, and he would be forever grateful.

He stopped, experiencing a rush of anguish because the old guy was gone. And his house was gone. Women he had loved were out of his life forever. The last time he'd come in search of wood had been with his wife. Ex-wife. After loading the truck, they had stopped at dark in a meadow for a beer and sandwiches. While a full moon was rising, she stripped off her clothes and danced around in the moonlight, spunky and happy and arrogant. She had a voluptuous body. He watched her for a while, then ambled into the meadow

and tackled her; they made love in the damp
and icy grass. No stars twinkled because the
entire sky had been made radiant by cascades
of lunar illumination.

Twenty-seven

The bird season ended on the final day of September. All the snow had melted, and he could hike back into the hills. He had no taste for killing, but brought along a gun. The aspens were at full fire, entire mountains flaming yellow, as gaudy as he'd ever seen. His heart felt more shaky than usual, and so he proceeded with extra caution. He carried the lightweight L.C. Smith to take a load off. No camera or extra clothes weighed down his pack, only a few shells, a sandwich, a small canteen. He advanced a hundred yards, stopped and breathed deeply to halt the arrhythmia, then cranked it up again. Today for sure he believed the hunting might kill him, but he could not think of a better way to die. *If it has to happen, let's hope it happens in the hills.*

He retraced the steps of one of his outings with the girl. He returned to a clearing where they had made love and sat on a log contemplating the grasses, which were still matted from where their bodies had been. The canopy overhead was a halo of golden leaves. And nothing much had changed. Smells were the same, the rot of damp moss, the grasses, wood bark, dying leaves, a faint odor of the sheep herd that had grazed through a few weeks ago.

He wanted to push higher than he'd ever gone before. The old logging roads narrowed as he climbed; the aspen trees seemed younger. He shuffled through gilded tunnels, stopping, starting, stopping again. His heart thundered. He breathed deeply to maintain control and laughed at his predicament. *Boy oh boy*, he sure felt mighty frail.

By and large, the forest was silent. Every now and then a red squirrel chattered, or a chickadee peeped. Juncos flitted invisibly inside protective spruce branches. He startled a doe eating grass at a little spring; she was not at all afraid. Then four elk—three cows and a large bull—clattered across the path and rumbled into the pines cracking dry branches underfoot.

The higher he went, the more intriguing his

forest seemed. He picked up a grouse tail feather and stuck it in the hair behind his ear. He figured he must be near eleven thousand feet. It was irresponsible to push any higher, though he still had a way to go. To get where? And "irresponsible" measured against what value system? He did not know. He simply had a strong desire to forge on. He had an almost pathological aversion to retreating, even though that was where safety lay.

He paused over a big black pile of fresh bear shit; that gave him a thrill. He sat at the edge of the overgrown road, huffing and puffing, happy and excited. A break in the trees revealed a panorama of golden hillsides across the canyon. A hawk drifted along the bright blue sky.

He resumed his climb. Mount Everest could have been no more difficult. Take one step, rest, take another step, relax, catch your breath, advance another foot. "You're crazy, man. If you drop dead way up here, nobody will ever find you." Good. There was beauty in that. He almost wished for it. Let the coyotes and the jays and the ravens pick clean his bones. Allow him in death, at least, to break away from civilization. It seemed anathema to die in the city.

Two grouse fluttered up from behind a log only twenty feet away. They took him completely by surprise and were long gone before he even thought to raise the gun. A few leaves and a breast feather dawdled down to earth.

Well, that was that. Normally, you only had

one chance on any given afternoon. He shed his pack and sat on the log, sipped water, and ate half his sandwich. Abruptly, his heart went truly crazy, totally out of control. He almost blacked out, slumped off the log, and lay in the middle of the old road, dizzy, nauseated, frightened. He gasped, strained to perform the Valsalva maneuver, but nothing worked. For about ten minutes it seemed like curtains. But gradually the old ticker quieted down. All his internal equipment relaxed; peace reassured his bones and muscles. Yet he remained immobile, eyes closed, resting.

Then, quite vividly, he remembered little Maria in a white dress high above the awestruck peasants, convinced that she would live forever.

Metaphors, he thought. He was light-headed and floating in a strange euphoria. I'm almost helpless, surrounded by a billion trees and many wild animals in the middle of nowhere. How silly. I really don't know why we do things, but we do them, and our persistence is remarkable. And in the next moment my heart—

Suddenly, he had a terrible longing to make love with that girl again and promise her everything.